Pieces of Truth

Ariena Vos

PIECES OF THE TRUTH
Copyright © 2021 by Ariena Vos

Print ISBN: 978-1-4866-2094-4
eBook ISBN: 978-1-4866-2095-1

Word Alive Press
119 De Baets Street, Winnipeg, MB R2J 3R9
www.wordalivepress.ca

WORD ALIVE
—P R E S S—

Cataloguing in Publication may be obtained through Library and Archives Canada

Contents

	Acknowledgements	v
	Preface	ix
1.	Dreams and Reality	1
2.	The Difference Between Me and You	16
3.	Just for a Moment	24
4.	This Piece of Me I Gave to You	40
5.	This Is Who We Are	56
6.	What Happened to Hope?	66
7.	Broken Hearts and Empty Promises	82
8.	What Happened to Goodbye?	98
9.	Your Secret, My Breaking Point	107
10.	This Isn't What I Want Anymore	116
11.	Please Don't Leave Me	126
12.	A Toast to New Beginnings	146
	About the Author	153

Acknowledgements

When I sat down to write this novel, and when I began the publishing process, I didn't think writing the acknowledgements would be the hardest part. The truth is, there are so many people who have supported me over the years and made this book possible. I wish I could talk about each and every one of them, but then this might be longer than the actual book, so let me thank the most important people.

Writing has always been a passion of mine, and this has been my dream for so long. Without these people, this story would still be a Word document.

Thank you to everyone in my family for always being there for me, for being my motivation, and for raising me in this amazing Catholic faith. Thank you for teaching me those values, traditions, and practices that make me a Catholic, and someone who can share these aspects of my story. Thank you to my awesome friends who inspired me, supported me, and gave me ideas. Thank you for helping me to write even when I didn't want to.

Thank you so much to Evan Braun, my absolutely amazing editor. Thank you for all the time and effort you put into editing and fixing my story… for all your ideas and suggestions that transformed my book, and for letting my story remain my story. Thank you for everything you have taught me that has helped me to grow as a writer.

Thank you to Jen Jandavs-Hedlin, my project manager/co-ordinator, for taking a chance on me and making this possible.

Thank you to my cover designer, who made me a beautiful cover with no more direction than "lots of colour" and the basic idea of the story. You did an amazing job!

Thank you to everyone at Word Alive Press who worked hard to make a dream become a reality and a real book.

Thank you to my mother, who was my number one inves-tor. Without you, I never would have made it this far. Thank you for believing in me enough to contribute in a huge way and giving me the opportunity to share my voice and ideas with the world.

Thank you to my great-grandma Frieda, who passed her love of reading and writing onto my mother, and onto me. Thank you for planting that seed in me, and for teaching me and my mother the power and joy that comes from a story. I know she would be proud to see this.

Finally, thank you to my support system. Thank you to my friends who gave me ideas and inspiration. Thank you to my very first reader, who gave me the courage to send in my manuscript. Thank you to the people who patiently listened to my rants when I ran into problems that seemed unfixable, and writers block that seemed impossible to get past. Thank you also to the people who taught me how to take constructive criticism, and all the people who gave me strength, love, and support. I couldn't have done this without any of you.

Preface

I don't pretend to be an expert on pain. I wrote this story because I think pain, love, and emotion are all very important. They go hand and hand. You can't have pain without love, you can't have love without pain, and you need emotion for both.

I wanted to show that we all go through these things, and they are hard, and they can seem impossible, and we sometimes just don't know what to do. And yes, sometimes we just want to give up.

But we don't have to.

As human beings, we revolve around love. We can't do anything without love—and that's the heart of this story. My motivation for writing this book was to express that emotion, to write about what happens when everything is going wrong and nothing is okay, when you don't know what to do. I wrote this so that my readers could relate to that experience and realize that, yes, we are strong and independent people.

And yet we can't do everything on our own. Sometimes we need help and support.

My experience writing this book was emotional, as some of the subjects addressed in it are heavy and intense. We see two different forms of loss throughout the story, and both of them are hard to deal with.

But through the process of writing this book, I also learned things about myself. I hope, through this book, you will learn about yourself too.

Chapter One

Dreams and Reality

"I WISH YOU WOULD JUST GO AWAY! STOP DOING THIS TO ME! JUST LET me live my life so you can live yours! I can't keep doing this with you! Just make it stop! Make all this stop!"

Emilio was shouting at me, throwing his fists in the air and yelling louder with each statement. Meanwhile I sobbed, shouting back at him and releasing all the emotion that had welled up in me.

"Do you think I wanted things to happen this way?" I said. "Do you think I wanted this to happen? No! Things just got way out of control and I'm sorry. I'm sorry, Emilio, okay? Everything just got away from us, but I can fix it! Just give me a chance!"

The rain came down harder, slashing at us. It was late afternoon now and the downpour had created a heavy mist thick enough that I could feel the perspiration tingling against my skin. I could smell the smell of fresh rain all around me.

We stood there on the sidewalk that was usually reserved for bikers, because it went all the way around town. We had stopped here, halfway to the park. All around us, big, pretty trees hung down; they looked stunning in the fall with the sky big and open above.

His next words were like fire shooting from his lips, so powerful that they burned every part of me: "I don't know how you planned this out, how you wanted it to work, but it didn't! I don't even care if you're sorry. Just leave me alone! I'm so sick and tired of you dragging me into all your drama! If you could fix it, you would have a long time ago! Forget it. I don't want to hear whatever else you have to say. I am so done with you!"

I felt a surge of panic, of desperation, and my words came out with more emotion than I intended. "No! Please, Emilio… please! Don't do this! Don't end it this way!"

I sobbed, shivering as the cold and rain mixed together, a kind of cold that even my raincoat and boots couldn't keep out. Couldn't keep away.

I ripped my hands out of my pockets and grabbed his arm as he started to turn away.

"Don't!" he shouted, anger sizzling in his eyes. "Leave. Me. Alone."

Then he wrenched his arm out of my grasp so hard that I lost balance and fell onto the sidewalk. When I looked up, I could see he was startled, and I felt bad.

He was about to reach out and help me when he shook his head and turned around, walking fast down the sidewalk.

I screamed, anger boiling up inside me. Anger at him, anger at myself, anger at the world.

Shakily, I pushed myself up and looked into the sky, raindrops falling onto my blotchy red face. I knew God was up there somewhere, watching me. He had let Emilio walk away, let him scream and yell and destroy me. How could God have done that to me? What had I ever done to God that He would punish me like this?

I closed my eyes and wrapped my arms around myself, praying I would open my eyes again and find that this was all a dream. That none of this had ever happened.

But when I opened my eyes, I was still there on the path, dripping wet, shaking, and crying. The wind slashed at me cruelly, taking the last bit of calm I had left in me.

It was over.

But how could it be over? I thought back to every moment I'd ever spent with Emilio, every time I'd felt a burst of happiness or joy or felt on top of the world because I loved him so much. I remembered the exhilaration that had filled my body when I stood beside him. All the things. All the times. All the memories. They played through my mind over and over like a movie that never stopped, thumping through me like a second heartbeat.

I burst into a full-blown sprint, running and running until I was home. I didn't want to think anymore. I couldn't think anymore. The only thing I wanted was to be alone. If I could do that, I would be happy. So I pushed and pushed, blocking everything out.

When I reached my house, I took a few deep breaths, trying to compose myself. If I could just contain my feelings until I was alone, I would be fine.

Once inside, I kicked off my boots and shrugged off my coat, leaving them in a heap on the floor, and made a beeline for the bathroom. I was so cold I could barely think. I turned on the steam and let it overtake me, relaxing my muscles and easing my mind. It didn't take the pain away, but it eased it for a little while.

That was the last time I ever saw Emilio Eastman.

Only a couple of days after our fight, Emilio was driving home with a bunch of his friends. They were laughing and having a great time, everyone distracted and high-fiving each other. Then the one who was driving got a phone call, and he started fighting with the guy sitting next to him since it was someone they both knew. The driver wasn't paying attention to the road and only took his hands off the steering wheel for a second…

The car sped off the road, rolled, and crashed into a tree. They were all in really bad shape, and the story was on the news for days.

Emilio was the only one who didn't survive. The emergency crews never found him, and after a long search they assumed his body was burned in the wreckage, something no one could have survived.

A week had passed since that fateful day, but to me it still felt like yesterday. Nobody had seen it coming. The thing that tortured me most is that my last memory of him was the crazy fight when we'd broken up. I had hated him that day.

I couldn't think about it too long, or I would go crazy.

I sat on my bed and stared at my computer, where I had a list of online classes and assignments. Most of them were quick and easy, and I could have done them in a second, but instead I closed the app and walked over to my closet. On the top shelf, I had a special box I had been filling since the day I had told Emilio I liked him. I gently placed it on the floor and began digging through its contents, flipping through photos of him, of us, and things I had made, like the pro/con list from the very beginning, a list of all the stupid things I had done around him, etc.

But way at the bottom was one of my most special treasures: a necklace with a silver heart-shaped locket with diamonds around the edges. I opened it up and inside were my two favourite pictures of us, one of us kissing and another with his arms around me. Engraved on the back in swirly letters were the words "I love you." He had given it to me on the day he'd told me he loved me. I had worn it every day, no matter what—until the beginning of the week when everything had started to crumble.

"Hello? Cadence, are you in here?"

Someone knocked on the door, then pushed it open. At first I thought it was my mom, since it was always my mom. I'd never really known my dad, since he had left when I was three. And I'd never understood why he left either; my mom refused to talk about him. That always used to bother me. But after losing Emilio, I could understand why it was so hard for her. It hurt to talk about the people we loved who weren't around anymore.

Still, I wasn't willing to share this with her, so I started trying to stuff my memory back in the box.

Then I recognized the voice as Ashley, my best friend, and I spread the items back out across the floor again. She was the only one who knew about this box and I wanted to keep it that way.

"Yes, I'm here," I called. "You can come in."

Ashley shut the door behind her and sighed when she saw all the keepsakes spread out around me. She had always been a bit prettier than me, with her short, wavy brown hair and sparkling blue eyes. Her tall, thin frame always showed off the bright colours she liked to wear.

I, on the other hand, had long straight blonde hair, chocolate brown eyes, and short skinny frame.

"Hey, what happened?" Ashley asked gently, taking a seat beside me. "Why are you looking at all this stuff?"

I sniffled, closed the locket, and put it back in the box.

"I'm pulling it all out so I can rip it apart," I said. "So I can burn it all, get rid of it, and forget I ever had it. I don't want to see it ever again."

I stared down at one particular photo and started to rip it—

But Ashley grabbed the photo from me before I had a chance to really damage it. She then moved some other items out of my reach and put her arms around me.

"Don't do that, okay? You love this stuff! Why would you want to burn it?"

I put my head in my hands, ready to cry, but only a few tears came out. This made me even more upset. Why couldn't I cry? What was wrong with me?

"I'm burning it because I don't want to see it anymore! Emilio is gone. He's dead, Ash, and I can't stop thinking about the last time I saw him... the last thing I said to him before he was gone forever... and I'll never be able to take it back. I'll never be able to make things right! Don't you see how torturous that is?"

Ashley was silent for a while, and then she started picking up my stuff. "Well, I'm not going to let you burn it. I'll take it home and keep it until you're ready to take it back." Her tone of voice suddenly perked up. "Now, I know your upset, so I have the perfect thing for us to do!"

I lifted my head at that, curious as to what she thought could possibly make this better.

"Tonight is musical adoration at church," she reminded me. "We should go!"

"Why would I want to go spend time with God after He did something like this to me? He let this happen, and it was horrible."

Ashley crossed her arms and sighed. "Cadence, that's a horrible thing to say! You should go spend time with God because it will make you feel better. He died on the cross so He could understand what it's like to go through pain, so He could be the one who understands when no one else does. Trust me, praying about it will make you feel so much better!"

"Forget it, Ash. I'll go next time," I muttered, avoiding her gaze.

She sighed and then stood up, tucking the last of the keepsakes into the box. She gave me a small smile and left with the box.

After she's done, I remained on the floor. All I wanted to do was cry, but no tears came. I didn't really feel anything. It felt like I was watching the world but wasn't really a part of it; I was just watching from a distance.

I put on my headphones, grabbed my computer, and kept myself distracted for the next week so I wouldn't have to be alone with my thoughts.

***

Now that it was summer, I spent lots of time outside, riding my bike along the cemented paths, letting the warm breezes cool me off and the bright sun shine down on me. I loved going to the expensive part of town, with the nicely landscaped yards and front walkways bursting with colourful flowers that filled the air with the faint smell of perfume. When I wasn't riding my bike, I climbed the trees by the park; the bark was rough on my legs but they offered me shade from the heat of summer.

After a week, I didn't feel any better. In fact, I felt angrier at the world than ever.

So when Ashley came back over to my house and again asked if I wanted to come to church, I agreed to it. The two of us were soon walking down the church steps at twilight after a refreshing service.

"Thanks for inviting me," I said as we sat on the steps. "It was really nice. I haven't done it in a while."

She smiled. "You're welcome. I'm just glad you finally forgave the Lord, and that you're happy again. And I hope you'll take back your Emilio box!"

She said it brightly, like she had just fixed everything.

I coughed and started fiddling with my charm bracelet. I threw down my hands, avoiding her gaze.

"It's not over yet, is it?" she asked, sounding slightly annoyed.

"Things aren't going to get back to the way they were before, and there's nothing anyone can do about it. It's over!"

"Okay, okay, you don't have to yell at me! I understand."

I shook my head, stood up, and paced around the steps, laughing bitterly.

She bit her lip and looked like she was about to cry. "I really do understand what you're going through. Why don't you believe that?"

I could tell she was hurt; it was in her tone. But I was just so angry that I didn't care. "No! You don't know what it's like when the most important person in your life dies… a person you really cared about, a person who made you feel special and safe and beautiful… When we broke up, he took back everything he ever said to me. And then I lost him! I just wish you could be more understanding about that. You keep pushing me and it's not helping. I need your support, not for you to just expect me to be fine."

I ran my hands through my loose hair and stomped my feet harder as I kept pacing.

Ashley stood up, tears spilling over onto her cheeks. "You know what, Cadence? That is so not true. Remember when my mom died? I know what it's like. I can't believe you could honestly stand here, look me in the eye, and say those things. I know that you're hurting, but don't turn this around and say that you never had a supportive friend, that I never looked out for you!"

Before I could reply, she held up her hand to stop me. She picked up her purse and ran down the steps and over to her dad's running car.

As I watched them drive away, the only thought in my mind was that I had messed up again. Would I ever stop?

I sat down on the steps, this time facing the church, and paid special attention to the huge cross affixed to the outside with the figure of Jesus nailed to it.

"Why do You keep doing these things to me?" I said aloud to Him. "What did I do? I just want it to stop! I want this huge, gaping hole inside me to go away! I want my best friend back! I want my life back!"

But yelling didn't make me feel better. Yelling at Emilio, yelling at Ashley, yelling at God… when would I learn to stop yelling at everyone who cared about me?

I laid my head on my knees and let myself cry, the tears blurring my vision and pooling on the rough fabric of my jeans.

As the sky darkened, I stared out at the rest of the people making their way to their cars from the church, their faces illuminated by the streetlights.

But there was one guy walking against the crowd, heading towards the church instead of away from it. He'd probably forgotten his wallet or something. He walked casually, both hands tucked into the front pockets of his skinny jeans, his body bouncing a little with every step, his head pointed slightly down, making him appear almost shy. He was tall, probably somewhere around six feet, with thick, tousled blonde hair that went to the nape of his neck. It was hard to tell from here, but he seemed to have gentle, sea-blue eyes and full red lips. I was drawn to his eyes right away. They were like nothing I'd ever seen before. So gentle and compassionate, like you could tell him anything and it would be okay.

He smiled at me, and it lit up his whole face. He looked so cool and confident, but also kind and friendly. In fact, he reminded me of Emilio. As he came up the steps, his presence made me feel relaxed.

I was so busy taking him in that I hardly noticed when he sat beside me. He cleared his throat, causing me to jump. This was crazy. But still, he reminded me so much of Emilio…

"Hey, are you okay?" he asked. "I heard you crying and I wanted to come see how you were doing. I'm Emerson, by the way."

I sniffled. "I'm Cadence. And no, I'm not okay."

He smiled a little. "Well, at least you're honest about it."

I gave him a weak smile, trying to give off some sign that I really was okay and he could leave. It seemed to me the last thing he'd want was me crying on his shoulder.

We sat in silence for a bit before I realized he was waiting for me to explain what had happened. He didn't even know me!

But I felt such a draw to him and the words just tumbled out of my mouth before I could stop them.

"I'm just... having a really hard time with some relationships in my life right now. My boyfriend, my best friend... it's all just a big crazy mess and I don't know how to fix it."

I put my head in my hands, taking deep breaths and holding in the tears.

"That sucks," he said. "I wouldn't worry too much about it, though. If they really care about you, they'll forgive you. That's what friends do. And as for your boyfriend, just know that all of us guys are really just giant marshmallows on the inside."

I nodded, laughing a little. But once it died away, I let his comment sink in and it hit me really hard. Tears sprang to my eyes.

This was ridiculous. What was I doing? Why was I talking to this stranger, some random guy? But again I kept talking, because I felt this pressure, this need, to explain myself.

"Do you remember that car accident that happened last week?" I asked, avoiding his gaze. "With some of the senior basketball boys and some of the Grade Nine soccer guys?"

"Yeah, what about them? They were all mostly okay."

I shook my head, staring hard at the cement steps in front of me. I had nothing to prove to this guy. But I did. Somehow, in some way, I did.

"Not all of them." My voice broke at the end, and when I worked up the courage to look up at Emerson and saw the sympathy and realization in this gaze—the same look everyone gave me these days—tears began to run down my cheeks.

"I'm sorry," he whispered. He put a warm hand on my knee, sending a warm shiver through my body.

We were silent for a little longer before he started talking again.

"What brings you here tonight?" he asked casually, as though changing the subject might make me feel better. As though it had the power to change the past, to help move me forward.

"I came here to pray, hoping the Lord would help me out and show me how to make things better," I said. "I've been so mad at Him. I mean, He let this horrible thing happen to me, and… I just… I don't know."

"I know what you mean. I used to be this amazing basketball player, captain of my team. But I got a pretty serious shoulder injury. Now I can't play anymore. It was a pretty rough experience. And you know what got me through it?" He pointed behind us at the cross. "I found God. I learned everything I could, and I learned that no matter how big the situation is, or how angry I am at Him, He will always be there."

"But how did you do that when you were blaming Him for what happened?"

He smiled. "Well, think of it this way: when you get what you want, that's God's direction. When you don't get what you want, that's God's protection. You have to think of it as God saving you from something bigger than yourself. I wasn't meant to play basketball, and you weren't meant to end up with that guy. The only way to get past it is to trust that God is looking out for you."

"Wow, I like that," I said. "You're really good at this stuff. When did you learn it all?"

He chuckled and looked off into the distance.

I directed my attention to his hand on my knee and almost reached for it… but then I changed my mind and pulled back. What was I thinking? What was I doing? This was all wrong.

I tried to ignore his hand. I couldn't focus on that right now.

"Lots of time praying, reading the Bible, going to mass, and learning everything I could about God," he replied. "It really helped me. Personally, I think that giving everything to Him is the only way to get close to Him, and to build up a relationship. Plus, I have really great supporters around me."

Now it was my turn to smile. "Sounds like you got a lot of good going for you right now."

It felt good to have such a great talk, to feel so comfortable with someone even though I'd only known for a few minutes. It also kind of scared me. And I certainly didn't need any more reminders of Emilio right, but I enjoyed this feeling of being protected and didn't want to ruin it.

"I guess you could say that," he said. "And soon, you will too. Trust me."

I nodded, laughing a little. I was wracking my brain for something to say, but then my phone beeped and a text appeared on the screen. It was from my mom.

"Oh, I have to go home now," I told him. "My mom's wondering where I am."

His face fell a bit, but he quickly picked it up again. He stood up and held out his hand. I took it and let him pull me up.

When I was on my feet again, I was standing really close to him, and as I looked into his eyes I forgot about how upset I had been just a few minutes ago, how mad at the world I was. There was only him.

Wait, what was I doing?!

"All right. Well, it was really great to meet you, Cadence. Hopefully I'll see you around here again some time."

I smiled and nodded, but inside I was secretly shaking my head, fighting the urge to scream, *No!* He was a great guy. A really great guy, actually.

That was the problem. I didn't want another great guy. I just wanted Emilio back.

But maybe, just maybe, Emerson could help me find my way back to God.

Chapter Two

The Difference Between Me and You

"ALL RIGHT, ONE MORE TIME! REMEMBER, EVERYONE: CHANNEL THAT inner emotion. Put everything into this. We want to feel your emotion and your passion as we watch you dance! Okay, last time. One, two, three!"

My dance teacher hit the play button on her phone, and I closed my eyes, standing still as I waited for the entrance music came in. Singing and songwriting were my passions, and I'd been doing it ever since I was little. Recently, my mom had signed me up for dance lessons too, so I could discover a new angle.

I was standing in the middle of the dance studio, surrounded by my fifteen classmates. The studio was small but pretty, with dark purple walls that had the black silhouettes of dancers painted on them. There was also a shiny floor-to-ceiling mirror that took up the whole wall in front of us.

The teacher had lined us up in three rows of five, and I was in the middle of the second line. I took a deep breath, trying not to focus on the people around me. I didn't want to get distracted right now, and I definitely didn't want to him about *him*. It had been three weeks since that day at the church, three weeks of seeing Emerson everyone, of timidly and cautiously hanging out with him…

At today's lesson, we would practice dancing to three different types of music. The first had been upbeat pop, and now we'd moved on to something sad and mellow. We would finish off with the tango. I found the mellow songs easier to dance to, especially today; they was something about listening to other people express their pain that eased mine a bit. Just knowing I wasn't the only person in the world who felt lost, scared, and broken reminded me that I wasn't alone.

When the next song started, I turned off my mind and focused on the music, letting it flow into me. I felt like the person who had written the song. I let myself escape, just for a moment, and push myself hard, moving with a fire and passion I hadn't really experienced before. I danced and danced and pushed and pushed until my lungs burned and my legs felt like lead. But I kept dancing because it made me feel strong.

For those few moments, when I was lost in the steady rhythm and thrum of the music, my heart wasn't broken. The lyrics expressed everything I felt, but left so much unspoken at the same time.

I just kept dancing.

By the time the song ended, I felt better than I had in a while. That's when I realized that a lot of the dancers were staring at me. I blushed a bit at the awe on their faces.

There were only about a dozen people in my class, and I knew them all. I couldn't dance like them, though, since they had been dancing their entire lives and I had only just started.

But things were different now. And dancing soothed me in a way nothing else had yet.

Thankfully, my teacher clapped her hands, focusing everyone's attention back on her.

"Good run, everyone! A special shoutout to Cadence. Your performance was perfect! Let's all try to portray the same amount of effort as she did. All right, now to end off the class we're going to go over our partner dancing. So grab a partner and we'll begin."

Once she turned around, everyone started talking and moving around the room. I wandered, looking for someone who I wouldn't have to make conversation with.

Then I saw someone whose present totally shocked me.

It was Emilio!

No, Emerson. It was Emerson.

What was Emerson doing here? I wracked my brain, searching for some kind of explanation. But then I remembered an email our teacher had sent out that one of the male dancers in our group had dropped out and she needed to find a replacement for him. Emerson must have been that replacement...

Without really thinking about it, I walked over to him. Frustratingly, I found myself super nervous. My stomach was doing flips as I felt a mixture of excitement and nervous fear. It kind of freaked me out, because I didn't want to feel this way about someone else.

I took a deep breath and walked the last few steps towards him.

"Hey!" he said when he saw me approaching. He had a big smile on his face. "Do you want to be my partner? I was watching you, and you're so much better than I am!"

I smiled as I marvelled at how cute he was. I looked down quickly, squeezing my eyes shut and pushing it away. No, it wouldn't be fair to like him. I was still far from okay, and he shouldn't have to deal with that.

"Sure," I said. "I'll be your partner."

He smiled and took my hand.

This time, when the music started, I had a hard time focusing on my steps. I was so nervous about messing up. And sure enough, I stumbled, missing one of the moves. Then a second one.

Emerson gave me a concerned look and mouthed, "Are you okay?"

I nodded, swallowed hard, and took another breath. I had to get this right. But we weren't moving together, at the same pace or the same rhythm, and I found myself struggling to catch up. He was moving so much faster than me.

Suddenly, I lost my balance and slipped, landing hard on my side.

The teacher stopped the music and everyone turned to look. I closed my eyes and lay on the floor, groaning at the impact of my fall.

Emerson leaned down beside me and asked if I was all right. I shook my head and stood up, ignoring his outstretched hand.

I ran out of the room, down the hallway, past another class, until I found the main lobby of the building where I sat on a couch and covered my face. Hot anger coursed through my body. Why couldn't I just move on? Why couldn't I just be happy?

Because Emilio was gone. He was gone and he was never coming back.

"Cadence? Hey, what happened?"

Emerson.

I lifted my head to look at him, concern and worry in his eyes. I sighed and shook my head.

He lifted an eyebrow and sat down beside me. "Did I do something wrong?"

"No, you didn't do anything wrong. It's me. I just... I had... I can't stop being... it's like it's controlling me! I want to live my life again and not have this hanging over me. I want to dance with you and not feel like I'm drowning. I want to be happy again!"

Emerson was quiet for a bit, then took my hand. "You have to let him go. That's the only way you can move on and feel free. I know, you don't want to do that, but it's the only way you can free yourself."

His tone was gentle and soothing. I knew he was trying to make me feel better, but sitting here with him, being comforted, it just reminded me of Emilio. Everything about him reminded me of Emilio.

"I know," I said. "But that's the difference between you and me. We spend so much time together, and you're so nice to me, even though I'm a mess and lost... and it's so not fair to you!"

His hand slip from mine, and mine fell to the cushions. He stood up and I thought for sure he was going to leave. I really didn't want him to, but I couldn't blame him.

When I looked up again, he was sitting on the coffee table, right across from me. He took both my hands and bowed his head.

"You and I are going to pray together," he said. "I know you probably don't want to, but we *are* going to pray. I don't want you to feel like this, so we'll pray for strength to get past it. I don't want you to compare yourself to me, so we'll pray for love. And I really want to be your friend and help you, so we'll pray for courage. Courage so you can find what's best for you, and to take my hand and let me help you."

I nodded and bowed my head too. "Okay, let's pray."

We made the sign of the cross and interlocked our hands, praying out loud and ignoring the people around us.

"Lord Jesus, we pray here today for Cadence, that she will find strength in you to keep going, even though she's experiencing something horrible and is going through a rough time," he began. "Please bless her, that she will be strong. We pray that she will find love in You to forgive herself, and to know how special she is, even now. Please bless her, that she will be loving towards herself. We pray that she will find courage in You, courage to let me be her friend, and courage to let me help her, even though it might be hard for her. Please bless her, that she will be courageous. In Your name we pray, amen."

"Amen," I repeated.

We made the sign of the cross and released hands.

He stood up but didn't come sit beside me again. Instead he leaned on the armrest of my chair.

"Are you leaving now?" I asked warily.

He nodded, then gave me one last smile and turned back to return to the class.

Once he was gone, I continued to sit there, a little in awe of this person who had prayed with me. While I was thinking about it, I realized my anger and sadness wasn't as strong as it had been.

Suddenly I felt a tug on my dance shirt. I looked down and saw a little girl standing next to him. She had curly red pigtails, ocean blue eyes, and a frilly pink tutu.

"Excuse me, what were you doing?" she asked in a whisper.

I leaned down so I could see her better. "I was praying."

Her eyes were wide, and she looked excited. She couldn't have been older than five years old.

"How do you do it?" she asked. "Please?"

I laughed a little and gently tugged on one of her pigtails, making her giggle and clasp her hands together.

"You say what's in you heart." It was the truest answer I could think of.

She pulled a teddy bear from her bag and hugged it, tears filling up in her eyes.

Concerned, I wrapped her up in a hug. "What's wrong?"

She sniffled and pulled away. "My grandma's in the hospital. I don't want her to die!"

Then she started crying, burying her head into my shoulder. I hugged her tight, letting her cry.

When she was done, I held onto her shoulders and looked her right in the eye. "Listen to me. Don't worry about your grandma, okay? You have to be brave so that she can get better. I'm sure she will feel good in no time. You just have to be brave and believe that she will get better."

She nodded, wiping her nose with the back of her hand.

"Okay, I'll try. Thank you, girl. You're really nice."

A voice crackled over the intercom, announcing the start of the next class. The girl kissed the top of her bear's head and put it back in the bag.

"I have to go now. Bye!"

I waved back, remaining on the couch until she was gone.

The thought occurred to me that I could have told her I would pray for her and her grandma, or I could have prayed with her, like Emerson had. Just another thing I had done wrong.

But then I remembered how happy I had made her, and how she'd shared this really personal thing with me, a stranger.

I thought about her for the rest of the day. Maybe if I did stuff like that more often, I would feel better.

Maybe Emerson *was* making a difference in my life.

Chapter Three

Just for a Moment

A WEEK LATER, I WAS STILL HAVING MORE BAD DAYS THAN GOOD. To get my mind off Emilio, I decided to go swimming at the local community pool. It was hugely popular during the summer.

"Where are you going, honey?" asked my mom as I entered the kitchen.

I had my bathing suit on under my shorts and tanktop and my hair was pulled into a ponytail.

"I was just thinking about going to the pool for a swim and some ice cream," I said as I put on my hat.

She stopped scooping the cookie dough onto the pan and laid her hands on the counter. I sighed, knowing what was coming. She had been really worried about me since my fight with Emilio, and after he'd died she had been constantly trying to make me feel better.

"Are you sure that's a good idea?" she asked. "I mean, you going by yourself. Maybe you should call one of your friends. Like Ashley, or that other person you've been hanging out with." She frowned. "Well, maybe not him."

I clenched my fists. "What's wrong with Emerson?"

She sighed and picked up the scoop again, filling it with dough. I didn't know what she was going to say, but I had a feeling it was going to make me mad.

"I just don't know if spending time with another boy is going to help this situation," she said. "You should give yourself enough time to completely grieve before you jump into another relationship. I just think it's a bit soon. The last thing I want is for you to get your heart broken again."

I closed my eyes and took a deep breath, trying to figure out how to best make her understand what was I was going through without giving away that I did, in fact, like him.

"Mom, I need you to understand something. I can't get memories of Emilio out of my head! Those thoughts follow me everywhere, ruining everything all the time. All I can think about is the last time I saw him, the last thing I said to him… it plays over and over in my head until I can't think, can't breathe. I feel stuck and I need to distract myself from that… so sometimes that means being with Emerson."

Hanging out with Emerson had its ups and downs. Sometimes he made me feel better, but other times I felt guilty for being with him.

My mom gave me a long, sad look. Pulling open a drawer, she handed me a bottle of sunscreen. I thanked her and left.

I decided to walk, since it was such a nice day. I slung my bag over one shoulder and put my earbuds in, listening to my favourite music.

The line to get into the pool wasn't too long when I got there, but I still had to stand on my tiptoes to scan for Emerson.

He had promised to meet me here. He wanted to talk to me about something.

He probably wanted to tell me he was done, that he couldn't put up with me anymore.

While waiting in line for my turn to pay, trying to push these thoughts out of my head, I noticed a boy and his mother standing in line in front of me. The boy was about ten, jumping up and down in excitement while his mom dug around in her purse.

Finally, she released the bag, sighing angrily.

"I'm so sorry, honey. I'm two dollars short. We must have forgot those quarters on the counter. I'm sorry, but we're going to have to go home and come back another day."

The boy stopped jumping and looked up at his mom, tears filling his eyes.

"But Mom, I'm finally big enough to go off the diving board! I've been practicing my flip for weeks! And Danny and I were going to dive for sharks, because we're finally big enough to go on the deep side! Come on, Mom!"

The mother stroked his cheeks softly. "I know, honey. I'm so sorry."

The man at the counter called next, and the woman stepped up, handing him everything she had. The man counted the coins and frowned.

"Excuse me, miss, but this is only three dollars. Entrance is five. I can't let you in until you give me two more dollars." He sounded impatient and annoyed.

The woman sighed and looked at her crying son.

I suddenly had an idea. I pulled out my bag and fished around inside for money.

"Here," I said, putting two dollars on the counter. "Now she has five dollars. Will you please let her and her son in?"

The woman looked up at me, surprise and gratitude in her eyes. "You really don't have to do that, dear. We can come back another day. You should keep your money."

I shook my head, giving her a small smile. "Please, let me do this for you and your son. I would hate for him to miss out on all that stuff he wanted to do today."

The woman's eyes brimmed with tears. "Oh, thank you! Thank you so much! That's so thoughtful of you. Honey, what do you say to this nice girl?"

The boy walked around his mom and gave me a huge hug. "Thank you, nice girl! Yes! Now I can go do my flips on the diving board!"

He tugged on his mother's hand, pulling her along. She gave me one last grateful smile and followed her son.

"That was a really nice thing you did for those people," a voice said from behind me.

I jumped at the voice behind me, turning around to come face to face with Emerson. When I saw his smile, my stomach rolled and I felt really happy. It was the same feeling I used to have around Emilio when we'd first started dating.

"I'm trying," I said once we had paid. "I want to be a good person again and stop letting my grief control me."

I pulled out my towel and laid in on the grass between the pool and picnic tables.

"Well, that's good, because I have something to tell you," he said. "Yesterday I was at the library looking for this book I wanted you read, and I met your friend Ashley. I sort of invited her out here to hang out with us."

My stomach tightened at the familiarity of his words. It was just like when me and Emilio had first met Ashley. We had been out getting ice cream and she was the girl waiting behind us in the line. He'd started talking to her while I ordered for us. Since the two of them shared the same taste in ice cream, he then insisted that she come hang out with us while we ate.

Blinking back tears, I mustered a smile. "That's cool."

It took everything inside me to sound upbeat. I guess I just hated the thought of having to share him, of bringing him into my social circle. It felt like he was trying to replace Emilio.

"Right," he said. "Let's all meet up for ice cream later. Sound cool?"

He looked so excited that I didn't have it in me to burst his bubble. I didn't trust myself to open my mouth, since I was scared at what might come out. Instead I just nodded.

He gave me a thumbs up and jogged off to the gate.

I laid down on my blanket, letting the sun warm me as I suppressed the tears that threatened to come out. There was nothing for me to say. I should have tried harder to keep him at an emotional distance. I had tried to ignore my pain by meeting someone new, but in the process I had used him. I was rushing into it before my emotions were ready.

There was no one to blame but myself. I had done this to me. I couldn't even blame God this time, because I had pushed Him away. Just like I pushed everyone away.

"Can I sit here?" Ashley asked.

I supposed that I didn't really care who sat with me, as long as I wasn't alone. I couldn't be alone right now.

"Sure," I replied, sitting up and watching as she laid out her towel.

We sat in silence for a while as she put sunscreen on. I watched all the people in the pool and wondered what it would be like to be one of them for a day—to get away from myself and live in another person's mind and body. Just for a moment, it would be nice to be someone different.

"Do you remember when the three of us used to come here? Me, you, and Emilio?" I asked, breaking the silence. "We always had so much fun. Wouldn't you love to be that happy again? To have that carefree, lovesick, bouncy feeling bubbling inside you?"

She didn't say anything for a minute. "I do remember. You guys always had way more fun than me. At least, in the years of ten, eleven, and twelve. It was better for me when we were little… but I'm happy now. *Now*. I'm in a good place. And do you know why? Over the summer, I strengthened my relationship with God. I gave myself to Him and now I wrap my comforts and sorrows in His embrace. It's the only way to not feel so alone when you are alone."

"I wish you would understand that I really am trying, Ashley. Emerson is helping me, teaching me as we go in that gentle, kind way of his. Sometimes, after we pray, I feel my grief slowly fading. Is that what it was like for you? When your mom died?"

A sad expression came across her face as she recalled painful memories. "First of all, no. That's not what it was like for me, because I was on my own. My dad was too busy drinking and throwing away our money to care about my feelings, and my grandparents stopped visiting. My two best friends were too busy being in love to check in on how I was feeling. I spent a long time pretending. But at night, I secretly wrote letters to my mom. I wanted to believe she was still looking out for me."

"Ash, I'm sorry. I didn't know."

She glared at her towel and picked at a loose thread. "Exactly. You didn't know. Because you were too busy with your own feelings. That's why I vowed to never do the same thing to you. But you're not making it easy for me, Cadence. You never do! Everything is always about Emilio, all the time. Sure, we still hang out, but it's never about me!"

"That isn't fair!" I yelled, ignoring all the people who had turned to stare at us as we fought. "You know I care about you."

Tears welled up in her eyes. "You haven't even asked me how I was doing! In fact, I can't remember the last time you asked me how I was!"

I flinched, directing my gaze to the ground. She got me there. But surely, if I started now, she would forgive me.

"I'm sorry, Ashley. I really am. How have you been doing since that night at the church?"

She didn't do anything at first. But after a few moments, she swiped at her tears and sighed. "Well, I actually met your friend Emerson the other day, when I was at the library."

At the mention of Emerson, my gut roiled. "Yeah, yeah. A friend of mine. We've been hanging out for a couple weeks."

Now it was my turn to pick at a loose thread on my towel. I had to keep my emotions under control. Push them down, bottle them up, like I had been doing ever since Emilio's death.

"He seems nice," she said. "Pretty great guy. Don't you think so?"

I wasn't sure what she was getting at, but I decided to give her a straight answer. "Yeah, he's… he's pretty amazing."

He was. Emerson was an amazing guy. I knew that. I had always known that.

"And pretty good-looking, hey?" She nudged me, giving me a knowing look.

I rolled my eyes. "Yep. Pretty cute."

Her face fell, her playful smile replaced with a serious look. I shifted uncomfortably on my towel. Whatever was going on, whatever was happening right now…

"But you wouldn't consider actually dating him, right?" she asked slowly, a hint of anger flashing in her eyes.

I coughed, choking on the water I had started drinking while she talked. I felt my cheeks heat up at her question. What was she trying to prove? That I wasn't over Emilio yet? That much was obvious.

"Ashley…"

I tried to figure out what to say, how to string together some sort of an answer, some sort of an explanation. But luckily, I didn't have to.

"Hey guys!" Emerson called over to us. "Cadence, I thought you were swimming, so I didn't bring you any ice cream. Sorry! So what are you guys talking about?"

He looked so happy as he handed Ashley her ice cream. She smiled and took a bite.

"Oh, nothing," Ashley said. "I was just asking Cadence what she thought of this new guy we met at school the other day."

Ashley took another bite of her ice cream, looking at Emerson and shrugging as he sat beside her, sitting back on his elbows and giving me a strange look. It was like he was trying to figure me out.

I stared down at my towel, anger bubbling up inside of me. Where did he get off looking at me like that? Where did he get off, after spending weeks with me, acting like my new Emilio? Where did he get off making me feel special and important…?

Well, I had news for him. Yes, I was having a hard time. Yes, I was grieving. But he didn't get to treat me like I'm a problem he could fix and then toss aside when he was done.

"Hey, Emerson," I said.

He turned to face me, a huge smile on his face. It was the kind of smile that made all my troubles go away, just for a moment. Seeing that one look, that smile… well, I lost it. I picked up my water bottle and threw it in his face, soaking him.

Ashley screamed as she handed him her towel. "What the hell, Cadence!"

I dropped the water bottle by my feet, watching as Emerson wiped off his face and glared at me. He had never glared at me before.

"Cadence, what's the matter with you!" He yelled angrily, running his hands through his hair.

I knew they were keeping something from me, some sort of secret that I wasn't allowed to know. I knew I had no right to do this to them, but I felt like I had to. Because I wanted everything to go away. I wanted all my memories of Emilio to go away, and if all I had at the end of the day was myself....

"I like you, okay?" I blurted out. "I've liked you ever since the day you put your hand on my knee at the church and told me everything was going to be all right. I liked you ever since you first smiled at me, and for just a moment you made everything seem better. And I know how crazy this is, but I had to say it because you make the pain go away!"

They both went silent. Feeling angry, tired, and embarrassed, I just wanted to go home.

Emerson's gaze still hard. "Look, Cadence—"

I could tell by his tone that I wasn't going to get the answer I wanted. I had been kidding myself this whole time. Why had I ever thought that this boy—this wonderful, amazing boy— would want a girl who was mourning her dead boyfriend? I'd been a fool to think I could ever get rid of this pain by pushing it away.

Before he could finish his sentence, I shoved my towel and empty water bottle in my bag, stood up, and left the pool.

When I got home, my mom was sitting on the couch watching a reality TV show. The house smelt like fresh baked cookies, and as I entered the house I saw a pan with the finished cookies cooling on the counter.

"How was the pool, honey?" she asked, turning around on the couch and resting her arms on the top.

The look in her eyes was so hopeful, so innocent, that I just couldn't tell her the truth. I knew she just wanted me to be happy, to feel better. But I couldn't do that if I kept messing up every good thing I had.

So I shook my head, tears spilling over, and ran out of the room. I ran past the kitchen, past the bathroom, past my parent's bedroom, and went through the doors that led onto the balcony.

I closed the doors, locked them behind me, and slid down against the wall. I pulled my knees up to my chin and wrapped my arms around them, rocking back and forth. My pain demanded to be felt. As the cool breeze blew over me, gently wiping the tears off my face, I felt shame and hurt and anger in every part of my body. I cried until my voice was hoarse and my throat hurt.

When I heard a knock at the door, I took in a deep breath and unlocked it.

My mom pushed it open and came outside. She didn't say anything but placed two things on the table beside me—a plate of cookies and my Bible.

When she left, I sat on one of the chairs. I was so tired of being angry at everyone and yelling and losing people. Emilio was gone. There was nothing I or anyone else could do about it. The only thing I could do was learn to move on.

I opened the Bible, flipping to a random page. When I looked at the verse in front of me, I thought it looked familiar: *"Do not fear, for I am with you, do not be afraid, for I am your God; I will strengthen you, I will help you, I will uphold you with my victorious right hand."* (Isaiah 41:10).

I read that passage over and over, reading it until I had it memorized. I started to feel a little calmer, a little happier, and a little closer to feeling okay.

In books and movies, people often say that a person's grief never completely goes away, that it will always be there and that you need to distract yourself from it so you won't feel it. as I sat there in the fading light, flipping through the Bible, I couldn't believe that.

What did I believe? I believed that I would never stop loving Emilio. He would always be in my heart. But I was also believed that my grief would go away, eventually. I needed to be brave. I needed to trust God.

But I still didn't really know how to do that, and the person who had been helping me through it was gone. I would probably never see Emerson again. That small fact was somehow worse than all the other ones combined, making my heart feel heavy again.

I shut the Bible, my hands shaking. I wish I wouldn't have to feel this way anymore. I wanted to be done with it. I wanted my old life back, the life where Ashley and I were still close friends and Emilio was alive and everything seemed so much simpler. So much easier.

As I thought about this, I remembered what Ashley had said during our fight at the pool—that she had gone through a lot after her mother died. Maybe none of those times together had actually been easy. It had only felt that way most of the time because I had Emilio.

I didn't want to go talk to Ashley, because I knew she would still be pretty mad. I didn't want to talk to Emerson, either, because I had no idea what he was going to say about my confession. He was such a nice person. I didn't think I could stand it if he were mad at me.

Not now, anyway.

———◆———

For the next few days, I stayed in my room, alone, and worked on a new song. I kept a small guitar in the corner of the room by the window. I'd gotten it for my tenth birthday and taught myself to play.

Looking around my room now, I could see most of my own songs strewn across the floor, or at least pieces of them. Empty score sheets, full score sheets, lines and ideas I had randomly thought of writing about, full songs on thin pages of loose leaf…

It reminded me of when I'd refused to leave my room after Emilio died. I wrote four songs during that time. It had been my coping mechanism. Feeling sad? Write a song. Feeling overwhelmed? Excited? Frustrated? Mad? Write a song.

Three days after the incident at the pool, my mom decided I needed to get out of the house. So I went with her to get groceries. While walking down the cereal isle, picking the ones that were on sale, a little girl came up to me, her eyes wide and excited.

"That's the girl, Mommy!" she said. "That's the girl I was telling you about!"

The girl ran up to me, gave me a big hug, and giggled while her teddy bear dangled from under her arm. I didn't recognize her at first, until I noticed her pigtails. She was the girl from the dance studio.

"Hello! I remember you. How's your grandma doing?" I asked, patting her back.

She let go and gave me a hug smile, hugging her bear tight to her chest.

"You were right," she said. "She's all better now. I was brave, just like you told me. And I said what was in my heart before I went to bed, like you said. Now she's all better, and I couldn't have done it without you!"

She squealed, giving me a big hug again.

I blushed, looking over at her mom, who pushed her shopping cart over and started talking to my mom.

"I really can't thank you enough," the girl's mom said. "I didn't know what I was going to do with her. She was so upset all the time. She wouldn't play with any of her friends. She wouldn't eat. And she kept thinking my mom was going to die. But then she met your daughter at dance last week and, I don't know, something just clicked!"

She gave me a grateful look and I smiled back.

I got down on my knees so my eyes were at the same level as the girl's.

"Happy to help," I told her. "I'm so happy your grandma is better! Now, if you ever need me again, just come find me at dance class okay? I'll be there."

She nodded, her curls bouncing around her shoulders as she skipped back to her mom. They both waved at us as they turned the corner.

My mom and I walked in silence for a while. She shook her head, laughing every once in a while.

But before she could say anything, another little kid came running up to me, a boy of about ten. When his mother saw me, her face broke out into a smile.

My mom gave me a questioning look.

"Hey! It's that girl from the pool, Mom!" the boy shouted. He had a huge grin on his face. "The one who paid for us to get in yesterday!" He looked up at me. "Guess what! At the pool yesterday, I went on the diving board, the really tall one, and I wasn't even scared! And I mastered that flip I've been practicing! Then, when my friend and I were diving for sharks in the *deep end*, I won!"

"That's awesome, buddy!" I said. "I'm so glad you had a good time! You went on the big diving board? And you weren't scared? Wow! I can't even go on that one!"

His eyes got big and he had such a look of childlike delight.

"Really? Mom, did you hear that? Even *she* is scared!"

His mom laughed as she came over and gave him a thumbs up. As the boy kept talking, I listened as our moms talked to each other.

"I mean, it was so thoughtful of her to do that for us, and it meant so much to my son," said the boy's mom. "You don't see a lot of young people these days doing things like that, you know? So, thank you so much, really."

My mom said something quietly back, but I couldn't hear it. Whatever it was, it made the other woman seem suddenly very sad.

Before long, the boy was tugging on her sleeve and they were off, waving as they left.

As we left the store that afternoon, I couldn't help but feel better than I had in a long time. I had made a huge difference in these people's lives, just by doing one small thing.

I guess it's something we can all do, I thought. *The things that seem the smallest and simplest to us can mean everything to someone else. If everyone everyday did something small like that, we could change this world and make it even better.*

Just for a moment, I felt convinced that maybe I *could* change the world. One small act at a time.

Chapter Four

This Piece of Me I gave to You

DEATH IS A FUNNY THING. SOMETIMES IT'S EXPECTED, LIKE WHEN YOU have a terminal condition. Sometimes you don't see it coming and have no time to prepare for it. It's a complicated concept, one that can be hard to understand.

That's how I felt about Emilio. I would never get another chance to talk to him or make things right. So, in some ways, meeting Emerson felt like I was getting a second chance. We'd just had a huge fight, but if I stayed mad and waited for him to come around, I could end up losing him too.

I couldn't make the same mistake twice. I needed Emerson my life, maybe more than I cared to admit. I also knew it probably wasn't the smartest idea to cling to him so tightly...

After breakfast that day, I hopped on my bike and followed the path to the street where he lived. Once I found the house, I parked my bike on the sidewalk and stood in front of his house. It wasn't big, with two vehicles in the cement driveway, a car and a truck. It was painted dark blue and had a yellow door, with two bay windows in front.

No, it wasn't big. But it was nice.

This was it. This was my chance. My chance to make things right. I had to take it.

Taking a deep breath, I marched up the steps and rang the doorbell, standing awkwardly on the steps. My stomach was flipping around and I immediately started to regret the decision. What if I said the wrong thing? What if he didn't want to hear what I had to say? Or worse, what if he didn't care?

By the time he opened the door, dark thoughts were creeping into my mind, taking over my good judgment.

He was wearing a pair of beige khaki shorts and an untucked orange t-shirt. His smooth unruly hair was tousled and he looked tired and sad. I felt small, upset, and sorry for making him feel that way.

When he saw me, he didn't reach out. What if this was the end?

He opened his mouth, but I cut him off, tears streaming down my face: "Look, I'm sorry, okay? I'm really, really, really sorry."

I avoided his gaze as I tried to wipe away my tears. I felt so stupid standing outside on a Friday morning, crying in front of a guy who was mad at me.

"I know I messed up and I'm sorry. I'm sorry."

He still wasn't saying anything. It was over. I had lost him over a stupid fight.

I turned around and started to leave, and before I even made it down the front steps I heard the door shut. He had closed the door on me. He didn't care.

But when I was halfway down the driveway, I felt a tug on my arm.

He had followed me.

"Get rid of all bitterness, rage and anger, brawling and slander, along with every form of malice," he said. "Be kind and compassionate to one another, forgiving each other, just as in Christ God forgave you. That's from Ephesians 4:31–32." He loosened his hold on me. "I forgive you, Cadence, just like the Lord God forgave you."

I felt like crying all over again. Instead I wiped my hand across my eyes and sniffled.

"A gentle answer turns away wrath, but a harsh word stirs up anger," I replied quietly.

He smiled, giving my arm a soft squeeze. "Ah. Doing your research, I see. Good job. Well, Cadence, remember that: in Him, we have redemption through His blood, the forgiveness of sins, in accordance with the riches of God's grace. Ephesians 1:7."

I threw my arms around him, laying my head on his shoulder. He was surprised at first, but sure enough, he returned the embrace.

"I'm really glad you came back actually, because there's something I wanted to ask you," he said with a mysterious glint in his eye that made me nervous.

I hope it wasn't about what I had said at the pool. I didn't want to talk about that right now.

"What?" I asked, searching his eyes for an answer.

His face broke out into a grin and he tried really hard to stifle a burst of laughter. I absolutely hated when people did that, but when he started laughing, I started laughing right back.

Finally, he took a deep breath, composing himself again. "Do you want to come on a walk with me?" he asked.

I stared at him for a minute, not knowing what to think. But he was waiting for an answer and it was a nice gesture.

Hesitantly, I nodded.

He gave me a thumbs up and turned back to the house, running inside but coming back out just as quickly, a picnic basket in one hand.

"Right," he said. "Let's go."

We walked in silence for most of the walk, waving at people as we passed. Finally we turned onto a gravel road that would lead us out of town. As we walked into the country, the whole world was in front of us.

"Where are you taking me?" I asked.

He put a finger to his lips and shook his head. Apparently it was a secret, which just made want to know the answer even more.

After a long walk, we finally stopped beside a little stream by a cluster of trees. Emerson laid out a blanket for us to sit on and opened the picnic basket. Instead were two plates and some lunch.

"So let's talk," he said once we started eating. "I know we've been hanging out for two months now, and I've gotten to know a lot of things about you in that time. But I feel like there's still some important stuff about you that I don't know. And I think we should talk about that."

He waited for me to jump in, and believe me I wanted to. But somehow my mouth stayed shut.

"Can you tell me about basketball?" I blurted out. "I want to hear about your basketball seasons."

He raised an eyebrow, but it immediately changed into a smile. "Well, I got into it one day when I was out with my dad. I had just been through a hard day at school and he took me to the park. We were sitting on a bench and some kids from school came over and started calling me names and stuff. I had quite a temper back then. Before they left, one of the guys threw a basketball at my head. I caught it and marched over to the court."

"So what did you do?" I asked. "I mean, you didn't, like, hit them or anything... did you?"

"No, I threw it at the basket—and to my surprise, it went right in. My dad was impressed and we spent the rest of the afternoon shooting baskets. He taught me different plays, and different ways to shoot the call. After that day, I joined the school's team. Once those kids found out I was one of the star players, they were so mad. They all tried to join too, but in the end only one other guy made it. He tried to get me kicked off, but it didn't work. I had talent."

"That's kind of cool. I mean, not that the guy was mean to you, but that you discovered that you were good at basketball." I was sure he was done with the story, so I tried to prompt him to tell me more. "So you've been playing ever since?"

"Yes. After that day at the park, basketball became really important to me. Every time I played, it reminded me how I could overcome weakness with power. I practiced all the time. Nothing could stop me."

Tears welled up in his eyes, and I suddenly realized there was an important part of the story he hadn't told me yet.

"How did you get hurt?" I asked quietly.

He sighed, letting the question float in the air for a few minutes. "We were losing pretty bad in the second half of a game. In the last thirty seconds, I jumped off the bench and ran in, wrestling the ball from the other team, desperately trying to win back the points we had lost. But I was going to fast. My teammates struggled to catch up with me. I wasn't focused on anyone else, and that's why I didn't notice my teammate, the one from the park, lunge at me to get the ball. I jumped, getting as much air as I could, but midair, just as I was about to release the ball, he knocked me sideways. I landed on my shoulder. The combined impact of my high fall, the guy falling on me, and the awkward position of my shoulder caused me to tear the rotator cuff in my left shoulder."

"Oh my gosh, Emerson! That's awful!"

He glared at the blanket we were sitting on. "I was in the hospital for a few days, and the doctors did everything they could. But the last day I was there, while all my teammates were there visiting me, the doctor came to deliver the news. Told me I wouldn't be able to play basketball again.

"After that, I was angry for a long time. I started losing all my friends and I got into lots of fights. Even my own family didn't want to be around me anymore. When I was alone, I would flip through all my school yearbooks and the pictures in my photo album. I ripped the photos apart, screaming in frustration. The next day, I opened the album the photos were back. I realized that my mom had snuck into my room whole I was sleeping and taped them back together. She never lost hope in me.

"On my fourteenth birthday, she bought me a Bible and took me to church. Slowly, I started working through my anger and depression. She helped me find God. I still miss basketball, but now I have God, and Ge helps me get through it. I have my mom to thank for that. That's why it's so important for me to help you rediscover God. I know what it feels like to be stuck in a hole with no way out. It breaks my heart to see another person go through it."

I wiped a tear from his cheek with my thumb. "Wow, Emerson, I'm so sorry."

I felt like I wanted to cry too, but he just shrugged and took a shuddering breath.

We sat in silence for a minute, both of us taking in the story. The creek in front of us flowed slowly and the trees swayed in the breeze, letting in little bits of sunlight, creating a little dome that held us in our own little world.

"I guess I'll talk now," I finally said. "Any requests?"

"Emilio. Tell me about him."

Closing his eyes, he lay down on the blanket and put his head on the grass. I followed his lead, and soon we were both laying down, our heads inches away from each other.

I took a deep breath and started from the very beginning.

"Well, I knew him ever since I was ten when I was babysitting my neighbour's three-year-old girls. They wanted to go to the park one day, so I took them. I was sitting up on the monkey bars, watching them and singing one of my new songs, while Emilio sneakily climbed up in front of me. I didn't notice he was there until he said, 'Nice song. You have a beautiful voice.' I jumped so high I almost fell off, but he grabbed my hand and steadied me. I blushed and mumbled thanks. We sat up there and talked, only leaving when one of the kids needed help."

"That's cool. So that's how you met? Nice. What happened after that?"

"We started hanging out a lot... at school, after school, on the weekends. It was always me, him, and Ashley. We were an unbreakable trio. But I was always closer to him than Ashley was. He and I were thirteen when we first started dating. We were slow-dancing at our school dance, and maybe it was the music, or the way he held me, or the way he looked into my eyes so deeply, like he really cared, or maybe it was the perfect way my head fit on his shoulder, in that spot under his chin and between his neck and shoulder... well, that's when I first realized how much I liked him."

"What were some of the things you liked most about him?" Emerson asked softly, his eyes gazing up at the sky.

I felt my gut tighten up in that familiar, painful way that only comes from heartache. But I kept going.

"He was a great guy. Funny, caring, compassionate, fun... he smiled all the time and he used to sneak up behind me and give me these huge hugs, kissing my cheek. I would pretend to be annoyed but then laugh and kiss him back. He was so happy all the time, and when he talked about something he was passionate about, his eyes would sparkle in this beautiful way. When he walked into a room, I would feel like he would always be there for me. He even came to church with me every Sunday and went to youth group on Thursdays. We prayed a lot too."

"It sounds like you guys had a great relationship," he said. "But then, what happened to make him so angry with you?"

"About a week before he died, we started having these huge fights. He was blaming me for things, accusing me of ruining his life… I wanted to help him, try to make him see that I didn't like the way we were behaving around each other either… but he wouldn't believe me. He thought all of our problems were my fault, that I had brought this upon him…"

I swallowed, tears brimming at the bad memories. I didn't know if I could keep going without crying.

"Cadence, I'm sorry. You don't have to keep talking if you don't want to." He ran a hand down my arm.

I took a deep breath. "No, it's okay. I can keep going."

"So was that the last time you saw him? After that really big fight you had in the rain?"

I nodded. "After that, all I wanted was for him to come to my house and tell me that he was sorry and that he hadn't really meant it. That he still cared about me. That it wasn't really over. But he never did. I stupidly waited for three days. On the third day, I got a call from his mom. She asked if me and my mom could please come over. Her voice had this strain to it, like she was trying as hard as she could to put on a smile over the phone. We drove over as fast as we could."

"Wait... you guys weren't alerted by the police? Only the family? You had to hear it from his parents? That's weird."

"They told us that Emilio had been in a freak accident and had been killed. I remember every detail, especially the way her voice choked at the end, the way my mother stroked her back, how my father starting rubbing his temples, resting his knees on his thighs. I remember how Emilio's dad looked away, blinking furiously, how the clock stroke three. Three in the afternoon. I remember how my insides froze, how I couldn't breathe. How I started panting, gripping the couch cushions so tightly my knuckles were burning, how I squeezed my eyes and started crying so hard it was like a rattle through my body."

"Oh, Cadence, that's terrible." He paused. "Actually, terrible doesn't even begin to describe it. What happened after that? What did you do?"

"All the adults crowded around me, trying to coax my hands to uncurl, to open my eyes, to breathe. But I couldn't hear them, not really. Every memory I had of Emilio tumbled through me, until I was sure I was going to die from the immense pain. Finally, I released the couch and my body started shaking. My mom led me to the stairs and told me to come down when I was calmed down. I nodded and ran up to his room. It was exactly how I remembered it."

I was crying now, a hard cry that felt like it would never be eased.

Emerson sat up and helped me up, holding me in his arms and rocking me back and forth. "It's okay, Cadence. You're okay. It's all going to be okay." He kept whispering those words to me until I calmed down. "How about I lead us in a prayer? You can say one too, if you want."

I nodded and we made the sign of the cross, then bowed our heads, hands interlocked like they had been that day in the dance studio.

"The Lord is my rock, my fortress and my deliverer," he began. "My God is my rock, in whom I take refuge, my shield and the horn of my salvation, my stronghold."

I took a deep breath and repeated it, saying it slowly.

"I do not fear, for You are with me," I added. "I do not anxiously look about myself, for You are my God. You will strengthen me. Surely you will help me. Surely you will uphold me with Your righteous hand. You are my God. Amen."

"Amen."

Once we had made the sign of the cross again, I started to feel better. It felt like God had listened to my prayer, had heard us, and was answering our call.

Emerson passed me a piece of chocolate cake from the picnic basket and sat back, taking a huge bite.

"I have something to say," he said, looking nervous. "You're probably going to get mad and freak out, but promise you will hear me out, okay?"

I nodded, taking a small bite of cake.

He released a breath and shook out his shoulders.

"How bad is this news?" I asked, worried.

He put a finger on my lips and lowered his hand, indicating for me to be quiet so he could say what he need to.

"Okay. So, you remember when we were at the pool? When you told me that you really liked me, and you listed all these little things that made you feel good? You said that when you're around me, it makes the pain go away. Well, I have to tell you something about that. I like you too, Cadence. I like you so much, it hurts sometimes. I have liked you since that first time I smiled at you, since that first time we talked on the church steps and you opened up to me, a complete stranger, and you let me help you. I've liked you since that day at the dance studio, when I saw you express your emotions with such extraordinary passion!"

I was silent for a minute, just staring at him. Here he was, pouring out his heart to me, this boy who had changed me, who had shown me there was another way… this boy who I had thought I'd lost. This boy who had made everything seem just a little bit better, just by being around. This boy who had done everything for me.

I smiled. "Like I could ever forget that day at the pool. There were so many things I left out, like how your eyes calm me down, and how when you smile at me it's like I'm the most important person in the whole world. I could have said that your laugh makes me want to laugh too, because just the sound of you being happy makes me want to be happy. I like you so much, Emerson, you have no idea. You pulled me out of this dark place I never thought I would escape. And I could never thank you enough."

He placed his hand on top of mine, our cake abandoned and forgotten.

"We helped each other," he replied.

He leaned in closer, but I pushed him away.

"What's wrong?" he asked, hurt, and confused.

But I had just remembered something really important, a critical fact I could not ignore. "Emerson, what was going on that day at the pool? With Ashley and everything? Did you really just randomly bump into her?"

"No. I guess it's a little more complicated than that. I liked you, a lot, and I wanted to know if you liked me back without actually asking you. So when I was at the library the other day, I found your friend. We talked and she agreed that if we told you that we were dating, and she sat beside you and gushed about me, if you liked me back, sooner or later you would get fed up and admit it to me."

I blinked, staring at him. That plan was stupid, but also cute at the same time.

"But what about all that other stuff she said to me?" I asked, remembering how we had gotten into a huge argument about Emilio and our friendship.

He gave me a funny look. "I only told her to talk about me. Anything else she said wasn't part of the plan. Why? What else did she say?"

He looked worried and reached out to me, but I shook my head and put on a carefree expression.

"Nothing. It's fine."

As soon as I said it, relief crossed his face. I sidled up closer to him, close enough to touch. I didn't take my eyes off him, but before we could reach out to each other I broke off the gaze and looked away.

"There's just one thing that still bothers me," I whispered as I tucked a strand of hair behind my ear.

"What's that?"

I cleared my throat. "How can a great, wonderful guy like you, who's got his whole life together and got everything figured out light, like a girl like me who's struggling with so much grief?"

He didn't answer at first, but then he pulled me closer to him. "Is that how you see yourself, Cadence? Just a broken girl? You can't let that define you. Pain and fear only define you if you let them. And I'm just saying that to be nice because. There are many good things about you, Cadence, even now. Remember that boy at the pool? How you gave him money so he could go swimming? Remember how much that meant to him? You're still a good person inside. You just have to find a way to see yourself like that again."

"But I can't forget all those things Ashley said to me," I said. "I was so attached to Emilio, so caught up in my own happiness, that most of the time I wasn't there for her. When her mom died, I wasn't the kind of friend I should have been. And that's something she can hold against me forever."

Frankly, I was mad at myself for all those times I had ignored her.

"Well, she's not exactly being there for you either, in your time of grief," Emerson pointed out. "Look, if you let yourself drown in all the bad things you've done, you'll never be able to be the person you want to be. You won't let yourself be happy. I think you've been sad long enough, Cadence. It's time to let the girl you used to be come back into your heart. Everyone deserves to be happy, even you."

I hesitated, staring at the cool, calming water as it flowed gently by.

Everyone deserves to be happy, even you. Was that true? Maybe it was time to finally start believing that.

"But what about you?" I asked. "Are you happy? I mean, after everything you have been through?"

He had a far-off look, like he was thinking about the past two weeks. "But I thought you said I was a perfect guy who had everything figured out and his whole life together? I can't be both!"

I gave him a very weak smile. "You'd be surprised how easily people can hide their problems. Make the world think they're happy, joyful, without a care in the world. But inside they're actually dying, begging someone to see through the mask and rescue them from the heartache of whatever they've been through."

Emerson frowned, watching the small fish dart past in the river. The trees' reflections glistening on the water.

"That's terrible," he said. "Wouldn't you rather have people know how you're feeling than to suffer the pain and bear it alone?"

I shrugged. "Is that what you did when you found out you couldn't play basketball?"

The words hung in the air between us for a few seconds, neither of us moving. Then Emerson's face broke out into a smile. What part of what I'd said had made him feel suddenly so happy?

"You know what I think, Cadence? I think you're destined for great things."

I blushed, but before I could say anything he leaned forward and kissed me. I was surprised at first, but it quickly faded as I put my arms around his neck.

He traced his fingers down my arm, sending shivers of excitement and a feeling of happiness I had never experienced before. His skin was so soft and warm, and his lips were soft and tasted like chocolate.

I pulled him closer to me, never wanting this feeling to end. I felt so safe and happy and special, like I was floating on air, dancing on the tips of the clouds.

I moved my hands into his hair as he lay his palm against the side of my face. He made me feel so alive. It seemed as though nothing could take him away from me. The world faded around us, leaving us to luxuriate in these beautiful feelings. Warmth spread through my body, all the way to the tips of my fingers.

And as we kissed each other, bring out the best feelings I had felt in a long time, two things became clear to me. One was that Emerson and I really were going to be okay. Our pain had been felt. It was time for us to embrace happiness and lead each other into a better life. And two, I really liked Emerson and nothing was going to take that away from me, ever.

Chapter Five

This Is Who We Are

"ONE SCOOP OF CHOCOLATE CHIP COOKIE DOUGH, AND ONE OF caramel brownie please," I said.

The kid at the counter nodded, then grabbed a cone from the dispenser beside him.

It was the middle of July and Emerson and I had been dating for a month. Most of the people I met were happy for me, and lots told me I was so lucky to have a great guy like Emerson.

The only person who wasn't completely thrilled was Ashley, so I decided to take her out for ice cream, just the two of us. I was determined to spend more time with her and not make the same mistakes as last time.

"What about you?" asked the worker behind the counter after me my cone.

Ashley stared at the rows of choices, almost every kind you could imagine. After a minute of thinking, she pointed at two different kinds.

"I'll take a scoop of strawberry cheesecake and a scoop of blueberry delight." Blushing a little, she added, "Oh, and in a dish please."

The guy gave her a smile and pulled out a dish from the opposite side of the cones. He gave her two large scoops and stuck the blue and pink spoon in the top before handing it to her.

We waved and went to find a table on the patio, since it was packed indoors. This was the most popular ice cream parlour in town.

Once we found a small table out in the sun, we ate our dessert. We waited until we were almost done to start talking. I wasn't sure what to expect from her, since she still seemed mad. Things just weren't the same as they used to be.

I guess Emilio's death had affected her more than I thought. It was still weird not to have him around.

"Look, Ashley, I know you're still mad, but I just wish we could get past this," I said. "I don't want this to break apart our friendship."

She wouldn't look at me for a long time without saying anything. "I'm not mad that you're dating Emerson. I'm mad because it feels like you're moving on so fast. Emilio only died three months ago! You know, when you look at Emerson, it's just like the way you used to look at Emilio."

I could see the anger and hurt blazing in her eyes. "So what? I'm never allowed to be happy ever again? That's not fair. I loved Emilio! But I have to move on at some point. And if you were a supportive friend, you would be happy for me."

Not feeling hungry anymore, I stood up and threw out the rest of my ice cream cone.

Just before I left, she called out to me. "Cadence! I'm sorry."

I didn't turn around, just stopped, but I stopped. She was breathing heavily, like she was trying not to cry.

"I'm sorry too," I said back.

But I left anyway, dodging people until I was on the street.

Before I headed home, I looked back to our table and saw her sitting there with her head in her hands, her shoulders shaking. I felt bad for making her cry, but I didn't know what to do. Emilio's death hung between us. Instead of becoming closer in shared grief, it was tearing us apart.

I turned away from it, wishing the whole situation would just go away, and walked towards Emerson's house. The place had become like a second home to me.

When I knocked on the door, his sister Mia answered. Her face broke into a grin, making her look even prettier than she already was. Mia had these deep hazel eyes that made you feel like she knew exactly what you were feeling, just by looking at you. She had full red lips and a bob-cut hairstyle that started at her chin and went up to the top of her neck. Her usual outfit was black leggings and tight t-shirts, but on hot summer days she wore cut-off jeans. And you never saw her go anywhere without her charm bracelet; she'd gotten it when she was a baby and added a new charm with every birthday. Now that she was thirteen, they were starting to add up on the silver chain.

"Mind if I come in?" I asked.

She nodded vigorously. You could always count on Mia to be bouncy and bubbly. She was a bundle of energy and was always doing something new, different crafts and hobbies.

As we walked through the house, I tried to look into her bedroom. By the looks of it, she was trying her hand at painting on canvas. She was really good at it and I was pretty sure she could be an artist if she wanted.

Once we got to Emerson's room, she gave me a quick hug and went off to her own room.

"Knock-knock," I said, standing in the doorway.

Emerson looked up, startled, then quickly tucked away the magazine he had been reading and hopped off the bed.

He had an interesting room. Two huge signed baseball posters hung above the bed and his desk was always cluttered with papers and cards. Pictures were placed all around the desk and along the walls. A guitar stood in the corner.

"Hey! Wasn't expecting to see you for a while. Movie doesn't start for another half-hour. And aren't you supposed to be getting ice cream with Ashley right now?"

He gave me a look at that one. Ashley had been in on Emerson's feelings from the start, but that didn't mean she was happy about it. It had turned she'd only agreed to be part of Emerson's plan so she could talk me out of it.

Anyway, Emerson had made it one of his big goals to get the two of us to make up.

I sighed and flopped onto his beanbag chair. "I'm trying, but she just won't forgive me! She's still so mad about every-thing… and now I'm dating you and that's making her even more mad. I just can't seem to get through to her."

He was silent for a minute, then held out his hand and pulled me up. He kissed the top of my forehead and wrapped me up in his arms.

"It's all going to be okay," he said. "As long as you trust in God, He will lead you down the right path."

As he held me, I allowed his words to sink in. God would look out for me.

Suddenly, he pulled away, wearing one of his mysterious smiles. "I have a surprise for you! I was going to wait until dinner, but now seems like a more appropriate occasion."

"What is it?"

A smile spread across my face. You never knew what you were going to get with Emerson. He was crazy and fun and spontaneous. He always said life was better, and sweet, with little surprises to brighten your day.

"You have to close your eyes," he said.

I pouted and shut them tight. I then heard his footsteps cross the room. And a drawer opened...

He crossed back over to me and held out my hand, palm down.

"Remember how you told me about that necklace Emilio gave you?" he asked. "Well, I thought I would get you one too."

I opened my eyes and saw the gift held in his hand—a gold chain that seemed to shimmer when you moved it. It had a single charm on it, next to a cross in the middle. And attached to each side of the cross were our names.

Tears brimmed in my eyes. "Emerson, this is beautiful! Thank you!"

We sat on the bed and he started swinging his feet back and forth. He looked just like Emilio used to.

"It represents us," he explained. "You and me, brought together by God, staying together through the love of God, and never separated because of the love of God. This is who we are. Now you will never feel alone, because no matter where you go you will have me, and God will be with you too."

I didn't say anything at first; I just put one hand around his waist and gave him a warm, sweet, loving kiss.

When we broke apart, I smiled at him. "Thank you."

———◆———

After he gave me the necklace, we decided to skip the movie and just hang out at his house. When his mom pulled him away to help her with something, I went to hang out with Mia, who was in her room, working on a painting of three horses running through a field of flowers in the springtime. Her technique was perfect, with the breeze pulling back the horses' long manes, their hooves lightly hitting the soft grass as they ran, kicking up dust that rolled up around their ankles. The sky was fading into a sunset, the colours bleeding together. It really made the horses' colours pop. The grass was a rich green, with small, colourful flowers blooming around them.

"Cadence?" Emerson peeked his head into the doorway, his eyes immediately going to the painting. "Wow, Mia! That's amazing!"

"Man, between you and Cadence and Mom I'm going to have to go back to painting in the park," Mia said. "It's not that good. I can still improve."

Emerson rolled his eyes. "Well, of course there's always room for improvement, but that doesn't mean where you are right now isn't good. I wish you would take some time to just look at your work from our point of view and admire it. Let yourself feel good about it instead of always being so critical!"

She huffed out a breath and pushed her brush into a cup of water. "I wish you would just let it go. Let me paint the way I want to paint and look at it the way I want to look at it!"

He held up his hands in defence. "All right, sorry! Just saying. You don't have to be so hard on yourself all the time."

Mia grumbled as selected a new colour for the field of flowers.

"Is there a reason you're here?" she asked. "Or is it just to be annoying?"

He rolled his eyes and crossed his arms, the way he usually did when he was with his sister. They didn't always get along very well, especially when it came to her art.

"I came to tell you that Mom's done with me, so I'm coming to steal back Cadence."

She waved her hand, indicating that I could go.

"Do you want to bake something with me?" Emerson asked me as we left the room.

I nodded eagerly. Emerson was an amazing baker, and everything he made tasted pretty good.

The family had a really nice kitchen with a huge island, a stainless steel fridge, and a double oven. I took a seat at the island, in front of all the ingredients. He handed me the recipe.

"Caramel white chocolate chip cookies? Is that even good?" I asked, raising an eyebrow.

He threw a hand on his chest, pretending to be deeply offended. "Of course it's good! Do you doubt my expertise?"

He gave me a cute smile and handed me an egg.

After about half an hour, we were laughing and smiling and having a great time. That was the thing about spending time with Emerson; he was always trying to be funny, and his boyish excitement about everything was adorable.

"Are you ready for the official taste test?" he asked when we had finished prepping the cookie dough.

I stopped stirring and slid it over to him. He took a huge scoop with his finger and stuck it straight into his mouth. I took much less, earning a raised eyebrow from him.

"Excuse me but what was that?" he asked.

"It was me, taste-testing."

He threw up his hands in fake outrage. "That was the lamest, wimpiest taste test I've ever seen. You need to break out your sugar-loving spirit and take what you want, because this batter is amazing!" He took another huge dip and sucked it off his finger with no shame.

When he saw the look on my face, he stopped.

"What?"

"Did you just double dip?" I asked. "Getting all your dirty germs in our cookie batter?"

He wiped his finger off on his jeans and dipped his opposite finger in instead. But he didn't lick it. No, he put it on the tip of my nose, laughing as he pulled away.

"Emerson, come here," I whispered. "I want to tell you something."

I very slowly pulled the bowl toward me. He leaned close across the island, and I had to lean in too, scooping my finger in the middle of the bowl in the process. He looked like he was trying really hard to suppress a laugh.

"What's that, Cadence?" he asked, matching my playful tone.

I cleared my throat and brought my finger out of the bowl, putting a dollop on his nose too. We both burst out laughing. We laughed so hard that my stomach hurt.

He reached over to the sink to grab a cloth and rubbed the dough off me, then handed over the cloth so I could do the same for him. Once that was finished, he put a sprayed pan between us and handed me a spoon.

That night, Emerson walked me home. I held his hand, swinging our joined hands as we went. Under my arm I had tucked my share of the cookies. The smell wafted up as we walked, making me feel happy.

Our walk seemed to fly by. Emerson filled the time with jokes and fun. But when we were only one street away from my house, he led me over to a bench. We sat in the cool night air, watching as the first few stars peeked through the fading twilight.

"Was it really that bad with Ashley today?" he asked carefully.

I sighed, closing my eyes and trying to figure out the best way to explain it.

Eventually I gave up and just told it to him exactly as it was. "Yes. I don't know what I'm going to do! She's holding onto this anger so tightly, like if she lets it go she'll break apart. And I don't think she's ready to let go and pick up the pieces. I wish there was something I could do to fix this for her, but she just wants things to be like they were before."

I put my head on his shoulder, fighting back tears of frustration.

"You just have to give her time to figure out what she wants," he said. "That's something no one can tell her. It's just something she has to do by herself. If she cares about you at all, she'll find her way back to you. Just you wait."

He sounded so sure of that. I hoped he was right.

"Can I tell you something?" I asked, looking up into his eyes. "I've never met anyone like you before. You have this crazy way of thinking! Like no matter what, you're sure there will be good somewhere, no matter what."

He kissed the top of my head. "I'm not sure about everything, but I know one thing for certain: I'll never give up on you. No matter what. Ever."

And right then, as soon as the words left his mouth, I truly believed him with my whole heart.

What a mistake that was.

Chapter Six

What Happened to Hope?

"Emerson, do you ever wish that scientists left some things undiscovered? Like, those beautiful little mysteries God created? Take rainbows, for example. Before scientists broke them down and made them a force of nature, they were a promise from God. Now people don't see them that way because some scientist just decided that he *had* to know how they were formed! I wish sometimes those sweet and little mysteries could *stay* mysteries."

Emerson nodded, taking a huge bite of his burger.

We were at the bowling ally, one of Emerson's favourite places, and one we hadn't been to yet since we'd started dating. After playing a full game, we had stopped for a lunch of burgers and chili fries. We had one more game booked after this, and I was determined to win before I had to go home.

Emerson finished chewing his burger and swallowed. "You know what that reminds me of? Bubbles! They're so beautiful, and they seem like such a mystery. But a different kind of mystery than, for example, who murdered the man down the street. If scientists didn't break them down and make them explainable, they would be nothing less than gifts from God."

I stuffed the last two fries into my mouth, waiting to see if he was going to say more. He didn't.

"On a completely unrelated note, I'm so going to beat you in this next game."

I looked away, trying to look innocent. But after a few seconds, I snuck a peek at him and saw that he had his arms crossed on the table and a sneaky smile on his face.

"You really think you can beat me?" he asked. "The bowling master? The bowling champion? The bowler who can bowl backwards with his eyes closed?"

I slammed my hands on the table, rolling my eyes and shaking my head. "That was one time! And you didn't even get a strike! You hit one pin!"

He leaned back in his chair, laughing so hard. I lay my head between my hands on the table. I was a terrible bowler and we both knew it. Last game I'd scored fifty points. He'd scored *one hundred* fifty. It didn't matter how hard I tried, I just could not beat him.

He finally got out of his chair and took my hand. When I stood up, he put his arm around my shoulders and we walked over to our lane. Once we got there, Emerson re-entered our names into the computer and I started eating the candy on the table.

"Hey, I have an idea," I said. "Every time you get a strike, you get a candy, and every time I miss, you get a candy."

"You're on!"

We did a high-five and got ready to start.

Emerson grabbed the first ball and stepped up, preparing to throw his first strike. But he never got to throw it. I remember those last beautiful minutes between us like they were yesterday. After that, our entire lives changed forever.

His phone rang and he put the ball back in place, stepping onto the tile.

"Hey Dad. What's up?"

His voice was bright, his smile so happy and innocent. I don't believe he deserved what happened over the next few weeks. None of them did.

The call volume on his phone was loud enough that if I listened hard, I could catch a few words. In the end, I only caught two: "she's sick."

Emerson's face paled and he sat down hard on one of the plastic chairs.

"No. How? No, no… I understand. Yes, I'm coming right now. Bye."

He hung up the phone, shoving it in his pocket.

"Emerson, what's going on? What's wrong?" He was already pacing the floor, running his hand through his hair, muttering to himself.

When I couldn't take it any longer, I stood up and got directly in his path. I put my hands on his shoulders.

"What's wrong?" I asked again, looking into his eyes. They were full of fear.

"It's Mia. She's sick. Like, *really sick.* My parents don't know what happen. It was so sudden! They're on their way to the doctor but he said they would come get me."

I nodded, stepping aside so he could get by. I packed up our leftover food, a bag of candy and two bags of chips.

He touched my arm. "I'm so sorry."

"No, Emerson, don't be sorry. Your family needs you right now. Who am I to tell you not to go be there for them?"

He gave me a wobbly smile and kissed me, his soft lips full of apology and gratitude.

When he pulled away, I pushed him toward the door. "Now go see your sister. I really hope she'll be okay."

He nodded, waving one last time.

With Emerson and his whole family at the doctor, I had no choice but to go home and wait for him to call me back with the news.

Sure enough, two hours later, my phone rang.

"How is she?" I asked, jumping off the bed and putting the phone to my ear.

"She's got hypoxemia. It's a condition where you have low levels of oxygen in your blood. Apparently there are many different kinds, so she had to go through tons of tests. Eventually they diagnosed her with ventilation/perfusion mismatch, the most common type."

His voice low and rough. Not the Emerson I knew at all.

"Well, is she going to be okay?" I asked carefully, trying not to press him too hard for information.

"The doctor let us bring her home. Since it was pretty bad today, the doctor says she has to stay in bed. The goal of her treatment is to raise her blood oxygen levels back to normal." He sounded so sad, and so tired.

"So she'll be okay then?"

I knew I was probably driving him crazy with that question, and I should have been asking something more specific, but right now all that mattered to me was whether she was going to be okay.

"Well, she has to wear an oxygen mask when she goes to bed, but as long as she stays in bed and doesn't do anything to lower her blood oxygen any further, she should be fine."

I nodded, forgetting for a minute that he couldn't see my face.

"Do you guys know how it happened?" I asked, calmer this time.

Emerson took a shuddering breath. "They said it was a mixture of asthma and a blood clot in the lung."

"Oh my gosh, that's awful!" I cried, a lump forming in my throat.

He sighed. "Yep. The best thing we can do right now is pray for her. Can you help us with that?"

He sounded really desperate, and I knew this was about both of us—for God to hear his pleas for his sister, and to show me the power of putting trust in God.

"Of course I can."

———————

I didn't see Emerson for a few days after that. He called me sometimes, but he only ever had a few minutes before he had to go, and he was usually distracted. It seemed like his heart just wasn't in it. I hated to see him like this, so sad and worried.

So after each phone call, I spent half an hour praying for Mia, Emerson and their family, hoping more than anything that they would get through this.

———————

One evening I went out on a walk, trying to clear my head. Just as I was about to head home, I saw someone on at the end of the street. The person had a plastic bag, and it was tipped over so the contents were half-spilled onto the pavement.

I couldn't make out who the person was, but in a moment they had doubled over, clutching their chest. Something was wrong.

I ran as fast as I could, hoping to help them before things got worse.

When I got closer, I was shocked to see it was Mia.

"Mia! What are you doing out here?" I asked. "You're not supposed to be leaving the house!"

She moaned, trying to hide her hands from me. "Paint. I needed… I needed… paint."

Her voice was raspy and quiet, and she had a hard time talking. That's when I remembered the plastic bag and its spilled contents. Holding onto her with one hand, I bent down to see what was inside. Sure enough, it was tubes of paint.

"Why didn't you just ask somebody in your house to get it for you?" I asked, picking up the spilled tubes. "I'm sure somebody would have gone to the store for you!"

She looked at me sadly, like she knew something I didn't. "I couldn't. I had to do this on my own. I don't want to die, Cadence. I want to paint. I just want to paint."

She fell to the ground, sobbing and gripping her chest tighter.

That's when I realized that in our conversation so far she had been hiding her hands from me. I suddenly noticed that her fingernails were a faint shade of blue.

Quickly, I pulled my phone out of my pocket and dialled Emerson's number.

He answered quickly. "Cadence! Mia's gone! She's not in the house or down the street or outside! None of the neighbours saw her leave! We have to find her!"

"I found her down the street from the store just a few seconds ago," I explained. "She went out to get paint. Emerson, you guys have to get down here quick. Something's wrong!"

His breath was heavy on the other side of the phone, and I heard muffled voices, then someone else take the phone.

"Hi honey, it's Emerson's mom. Is she breathing heavy? Coughing? Have a headache? Blue skin anywhere?"

I took a moment to examine Mia. "She has heavy breathing and blueish fingernails."

More muffled voices.

"We'll be right over," she said.

I gave her the address and hung up the phone.

I don't remember much after that. Emerson and his mom came fast. She took over, prying Mia's hands away from her chest while I stood next to Emerson, squeezing his hand.

Tears welled up in his eyes. "I don't understand. Why would she do this?" he whispered.

"She said it was something she had to do on her own," I said, running my thumb over his knuckle. "She doesn't want to die."

He sighed lightly, more tears coating his cheeks. "Mia will be fine. She has to be fine."

I swallowed, not sure what to say to that. I wanted to reassure him and tell him everything was going to be fine, but I didn't know. The last thing I wanted was to give him false hope, make him believe with his whole heart that everything would work out.

But at the same time, that might be the only thing that could hold him together.

In the end, I didn't say anything at all.

Within a few moments, the ambulance arrived, its red lights flashing. The paramedics opened the back doors, picked up Mia, and attached an oxygen mask to face. They then placed some wires to her fingers to assess her condition.

Emerson's mom stood up from the sidewalk, brushing herself off and watching Mia sadly. We walked over to her and she wrapped her arms around us, pulling us close.

"Be brave," she whispered. "We have to be brave for her."

Emerson whispered some things back to her, but I wasn't listening. Those were the same words I had told the little girl at the dance studio when she'd told me about her grandma. Her grandma had gotten better, would Mia get better too?

But before I could say anything, Emerson's mom was climbing into the back of the ambulance. She waved at us one last time, then the door closed and took her and Mia away.

Once they were gone, I slipped my hand out of Emerson's and picked up the bag of paint. Silently, I handed it to him. He took one look at it and let the tears fall. I wrapped my arms around his neck, pulling him close.

"It's going to be okay," I whispered, my voice breaking at the end. I had to make him believe. He had to hold on.

"No, it's not, Cadence. It's not okay." He clutched the paint bag hard, letting it fall against my back.

"You can't think like that. You need to hold on to hope. It's the only thing that will keep you grounded."

He sniffled, wiping his face with his hand. "But what if I can't? What if it's too much?"

I pulled away from him, looking right into his eyes. "Listen to me, Emerson. You have to hold on. If you can't do it for yourself, then do it for your sister. She needs you to believe in her. Then she can believe in herself."

He looked away, brushing at more tears. I didn't know what to say or what to think. I could stand here and tell him that his sister would get better until I ran out of breath, but at the end of the day only he could let himself believe it.

Suddenly, I had an idea. I took both his hands the way he had taken mine last time. I made the sign of the cross and he did too.

"Dear Lord Jesus, we pray here for Mia, that she will have the strength to hold on and fight through her sickness," I began. "We pray that she will get better, and she will be able to paint for a long time. We pray for Emerson, that he will be brave enough to believe in his sister, and that You will guide him and his whole family through this rough time. Amen."

We made the sign of the cross and let our hands fall to our sides.

"Thank you, Cadence."

When he said that, I could tell he really meant it.

After I had prayed, I realized something: this whole week, I had been praying. I had been trusting in God. Emerson had helped me find my way back to God. Now it was my turn to lead him back.

———•———

Mia wasn't allowed to come home after that. She had to stay in the hospital where the doctors could monitor her condition. And although her mom was allowed to stay with her the whole week, the rest of us had to take shifts.

On my first visit, I tried to stay with Emerson. The key word there is *tried*. With everyone's tempers and emotions really high, I didn't seem to be wanted. I didn't even get into the hospital room to see Mia. Emerson yelled at me once, and after that I decided to go home.

I went into my room, closed the door, and got to work on a new song. I had gotten the inspiration for it from Emerson and his sister. It was about courage and heart and fighting for the things we need… fighting for things we had lost…

"Hey honey," my mom called through the door. "I just got a call from Emerson's mom. She said that Mia's asking for you."

I smiled, pumping a fist in the air. "Yes!"

The ride over was quiet, until my mom starting talking about halfway there.

"I just feel so bad for that poor family. An illness like that, so serious… it breaks my heart. Especially to such a nice girl like that one. Makes you think about who your friends are."

That made absolutely no sense to me. "What? What does that have to do with her being sick?"

My mother sighed, tapping her fingers on the wheel. "Nothing. Nothing, sweetie. It's just that… well, have you talked to Ashley recently?"

I groaned loud and long. Between my new boyfriend and Mia, I had completely dropped my old life. At least, that was how my mom saw it.

"I told you, she's still really mad," I said. "I've done everything! I apologized, asked about her day, took her out for ice cream, gave her a gift card for her favourite store… she just won't forgive me. Every time we try doing something, we end up fighting, I leave, and she sits and cries."

My mom glared at me. "Well, did you try just sitting with her? Just talking about it? That might help make her feel better.

You know what you could do? Go over to her house and ask for your Emilio box. I'm sure that will help."

I thought about that for a second, then nodded my head. Ashley had taken my box of keepsakes the week after Emilio died, to prevent me from ripping apart everything inside it. I still hadn't gotten it back.

"That's actually a good idea," I admitted. "If we look at some old photos, it might encourage her to open up."

She smiled and patted my hand.

With a few moments we had pulled into the hospital parking lot. I opened the car door and jumped out.

Once inside, I started looking for Emerson and his dad, hoping one of them could show me to her room. I searched her floor for a good ten minutes before I heard their familiar voices arguing by the cafeteria. I hesitated to go into the room, but I could still hear what they were saying from the hallway.

"I. Don't. Want. To," Emerson growled. "I'm not just going to leave her here!"

His dad let out a tired and frustrated sigh. "There's nothing I can do about it, son. If you love your sister, this is just something you're going have to deal with. The doctor said this is the best thing for her, and the only way she can get better."

Emerson slammed his hand on the counter. I didn't hear anyone scold them or call security. Then again, I figured these sorts of outbursts might be a common thing in hospitals.

"But she's only been here, like, four days!" Emerson shouted. "How can they possibly make a decision like that when she's barely been here? I don't get it. Whether she's here or there, it won't make a difference. She's never going to get better."

His father was quiet for a long time. I had decided they were done and was getting ready to sneak away when—

"Is that what you really think?" his dad asked, hurt and betrayal lingering in his tone. "Your sister would do it for you, and you know it. I can't believe you would rather let her die than move so she could get better! Now if you'll excuse me, I have to go find Cadence. Mia's been asking for her."

When I was sure he was gone, I skittered down the hallway. But before I entered the waiting room, I peeked back around the corner to see Emerson sitting alone at one of the plastic tables, head in his hands. He looked so sad that I almost went over to comfort him.

But I didn't have time.

"Oh, good you're here Cadence," Emerson's dad said when he spotted me. All hints of the recent argument were gone.

I gave him a smile. He motioned for me to follow him, and opened the door to her room,. Emerson's mom gave me a warm smile and offered me her chair.

"I'm off to get a snack from the canteen," she said.

She squeezed my arm before she left, giving me a mysterious look that I didn't know what to make of.

Once she left, I sat in the chair by Mia's bed. She was up and drawing in one of her sketchbooks, which was a relief because I hadn't been looking forward to having a one-sided conversation with her if she was half-conscious or asleep.

"Hey Mia, how are you doing?" I asked. I hated to interrupt her, but I didn't want to just sit there like an idiot either.

She looked up, and when she saw it was me her face broke out into a grin.

"Cadence! You came!"

She was still hooked up to an oxygen machine, but it was two wires attached under her nose so she could still talk. Her voice wasn't the same, though; it sounded raspier, and she spoke more slowly.

I got up and gave her a hug, careful to be gentle.

"Course I came!" I said. "But I am confused. Why did you want to see me?"

Her eyes lit up, like they usually did when she was excited or telling a secret. She started flipping through her sketchbook, passing pages of her art before she found the page she was looking for. Very carefully, she started to rip it out of the book.

"I wanted to paint this for my family," she said. "You know, before things got any worse. That's why I was at the store that night when you found me. If I had told them, they would have wanted to know what I was painting, blah blah blah. Now I won't be able to paint it. So I need you to hold onto it for me. Promise: if anything happens to me, you'll make sure they get to see it."

I hadn't even seen it yet, so I didn't know what to say—that is, until she handed me the paper, and suddenly I understood why. I had seen lots of her art, but none of them were like this. It was a family portrait, so beautiful and realistic that it looked almost like a photograph.

"Mia, this is amazing!"

"Thanks. I've been working on it for almost a year now."

I turned my attention to her, jaw wide open. A whole year? Wow. But looking back at it, I could understand why it had taken her so long. Her detail was amazing. All the little features of her family members were just right. And around each member she had drawn a little aura that represented who they were. She had shaded a sunset background, each colour fading into the next. Lastly, she had created a border with words that described the family.

I stared at a certain word that came up more than once, one she written at every corner: *hope*. Her favourite word. One that had so accurately represented her family before the diagnosis. They'd had an overflowing amount of hope…

Now it seemed like a cruel reminder of something they'd lost. Hope in each other. Hope in Mia. Hope in strength.

"I know what you're thinking. You probably don't think I'm going to survive this. I know that usually only one in 1,700 people survive extreme hypoxemia… but I don't want to die. I want to be an artist!"

She was crying now, tears wetting the empty page in her sketchbook. I put my hand on her hand, standing beside her bed.

"You *will* get through this, Mia. God will protect you. If you believe in Him, all things are possible. Especially recovery."

She looked at me, the twinkle of hope I had seen that day in the street gone. Fear had replaced it.

"Do you really believe that, Cadence?" she asked, twisting a corner of her hospital blanket between her fingers.

I smiled at her through my own tears. *Stay strong. I have to stay strong.*

"I have to, Mia. That's the only way you can get through this. I believe in you. Do this for you. Be that one person in 1,700 who survives. I know you, and you wouldn't give up just because it's too hard. This is your chance. Take it!"

She flipped her hand over, so our fingers were interlaced. "Well, if you can believe that, I can too. I realize we've only known each other for a month and a half, but I feel like we've been friends for a long time. I'm so glad I have you as a friend."

I sniffled, gripping her hand back. "Me too, Mia. Me too."

There was a knock at the door and Emerson's dad poked his head in. Mia waved with her free hand, offering a smile.

"Hey, girls. Sorry, Cadence, but your time's up. We need to have a family meeting. Thanks for coming and giving Mia a visit!"

I swallowed, disappointed and relieved at the same time. Mia gave me the picture, making sure her dad didn't see it, and waved goodbye. I waved back and ducked out of the room.

Chapter Seven

Broken Hearts and Empty Promises

"CADENCE, WAKE UP. WAKE UP!"

I moaned, rolling over. Someone was shaking me hard. The voice sounded familiar, but I was too tired to try and figure out who it was.

Mumbling something in my sleep, I rolled over again.

"Cadence!"

The person pinched my arm, their sharp nails digging into my arm. I cried out and sat up, coming face to face with Emerson.

"Emerson, what are you doing here? It's like the middle of the night!"

He put a finger to my lips, a desperate look in his eyes. Taking a closer look at him, I could see that he really was upset.

Not wanting to make him mad, I got out of bed. Was he going to take me somewhere?

I kicked him out into the hallway, giving me some privacy while I got dressed, then let him back in when I was ready.

"Okay, what's going on?" I asked.

"We need to talk. Come on a walk with me?"

I couldn't see him very well in the dark, but I nodded slowly. "All right then."

We walked silently through the house, stopping only to put on our shoes and sweaters. Emerson had to tie his runners, but I just shuffled into my flip-flops, throwing an electric purple hoodie over my T-shirt. He had on a grey zip-up sweater and baggy jeans.

He didn't say anything the whole walk; he just kept running his hands through his hair over and over. I could tell he was agitated, and I wondered if this had something to do with that argument he'd had with his dad.

Finally, after four blocks of walking, his silence had driven me crazy.

"Where are we going in the middle of night?" I demanded. "Nothing's open!"

He pursed his lips and stuck his hands in his pockets hard, refusing to look at me. "There is one place that's always open. We're going to the church."

I gave him a quizzical look, but he was determined to look anywhere except at me.

Thankfully, we turned at the corner and soon arrived outside the church. We didn't go in right away, instead choosing to stared up at the single light shining on the cross. The glow was strong enough that it helped illuminate Emerson's face. He looked like he was going to cry.

That's when I knew this was serious. Emerson hated crying in front of other people.

"Let's go," he whispered.

The door opened gracefully when we pulled on it, barely making a sound, and Emerson led us in. We walked to the middle of the sanctuary, genuflected, and entered the bench, kneeling to pray. From his back pocket, he pulled out two prayer cards, giving me one and holding onto the other. Then he made the sign of the cross.

"Dear Jesus, we come here today because I have news for Cadence that will be hard for both of us to bear," he began. "We offer these two prayers to You tonight before I tell her the news, a prayer for courage to tell the truth and be open and honest, and a prayer of trust, that we will leave this building still able to trust each other."

We bowed our heads and first recited the familiar words of the prayer for courage.

"O Christ Jesus, when all is darkness and we feel our weakness and helplessness, give us the sense of Your presence, Your love, and Your strength. Help us to have perfect trust in Your protecting love and strengthening power, so that nothing mat frighten or worry us, for, living close to You, we shall see Your hand, Your purpose, Your will through all things. Amen."

Next, we offered up the prayer for trust.

"O Lord, we ask for a boundless confidence and trust in Your divine mercy, and the courage to accept the crosses and sufferings which bring immense goodness to our souls and that of Your church. Help us to love You with a pure and contrite heart, and to humble ourselves beneath Your cross, as we climb the mountain of holiness, carrying our cross that leads to heavenly glory. Amen."

We lifted our heads and sat on the bench. I silently handed Emerson the card and he nodded in thanks.

He took a shuddering breath and looked deep into my eyes. Fear, pain, regret, and sadness filled his gaze.

This was driving me crazy. Something was wrong.

"Emerson, will you please just come out and say it?" I asked, placing my hand on his. "I'm sure it can't be that bad."

He laughed bitterly, swinging one foot back in forth above the carpeted floor.

"Please?"

I hated this. We could work through it if he would just tell me what was going on.

Emerson's eyes filled with tears. "The doctors, the ones that are taking care of Mia, they… they don't think she's getting the right amount of care here. So they want to move her to a new hospital. In Seattle. I'm moving, Cadence."

I felt like he had just stabbed me. It was like the day when I'd found out Emilio had died, when my world had been ripped away from me.

"What do you mean, you're moving? When?"

He sighed, running his finger over the top of the pew in front of us.

I clenched my fists, trying to control my breathing. I had to stay calm. This was hard enough for him without me freaking out.

"Tomorrow," he said.

I stared at him, anger ripping through me. Tomorrow? Emerson was leaving me in just a few hours?

He looked at me, silently pleading for me to understand. I wanted to. But it was the middle of the night and I was tired, mad, and heartbroken.

"How could you do this to me? Emerson, that's like six hours away! We didn't even get to spend your last day in town together. How can you spring this on me right now?"

I knew it wasn't fair of me to push him like this. He was upset enough. But right now, I needed to feel my feelings.

Tears welled up in hie eyes. "I'm sorry, Cadence. The doctor only told us yesterday. I tried to tell my parents that we couldn't go… that she could just stay here… but they wouldn't listen. They told me I was being selfish. I swear, Cadence, I tried everything! There's no other way."

"I can't believe you're doing this. What happened to you'll never leave me? That'll you'll never let anything come between us? That you'll always be there for me? What happened to that?"

I was crying now, throwing my hands up in the air.

He clenched his fists hard and glared at me, all composure lost. "That's not fair, Cadence. This wasn't my decision, and this wasn't my fault. Maybe we won't be able to spend as much time together as we used to, but I didn't break my promise. Come on, Cadence! I'm sorry this is happening, but there's nothing that can be done about it."

His voice was low and growly, but his eyes were tired and sad. I knew he didn't want to fight right now. But looking at him, it felt like I was right back on the street on that rainy day, begging Emilio to change his mind.

And I hated it.

"Well, maybe if you guys had been keeping a better eye on Mia, she wouldn't have left the house and gotten herself sicker," I said.

Emerson shook his head. "I can't believe you just said that. That is so not fair! She could have gotten worse even if she hadn't gotten out of bed!"

The heartbreak in his voice was strong. Watching his face, his anger, his desperation, I couldn't stop thinking about my last night with Emilio. Those memories were taking over my mind, every little thing that had happened… I remembered how he'd looked at me before he left, like I had ruined his life…

Emerson got up to leave. He shook his head and stomped out of the church.

Emilio had stomped away too. He'd yelled at me to leave him alone, then marched away, straight to his death.

I cupped my hands over my ears. *Make it stop. Make it stop…*

"No," I cried out, my voice breaking. "Please, Emilio, please! Don't do this. Don't end it this way."

I shut my eyes shut tight and clamped my hands over my ears, breathing heavy.

Nothing happened.

Then Emerson's gentle hands pried my hands away and I looked up into his eyes. It made me want to cry all over again. My lower lip trembled as I braced myself.

"I'm not Emilio, Cadence. You'll see me again. I'll come back."

I shook my head, scared to open my mouth. He couldn't promise that. Nobody could. Not even Emilio.

"No, you won't. Emilio didn't. I never saw him again after that night. He left without a second thought. How do I know you won't do the same thing?"

Hurt flashed across his face. "Well, I would do anything to make this work. If you don't trust me enough to believe, then I don't know why I'm still here."

With that, he got up and left. I held out my hand, perhaps in a gesture to make him come back, but he just kept walking.

I stood up angrily, taking off the necklace he had given me. It had always been me and him against the world, believing we could get through anything together.

Apparently not.

I ran a finger over our names and threw the stupid necklace across the church, not even bothering to listen for it to hit the floor. I sank to the ground as a nasty sob escaped me.

He was gone… he was gone and he wasn't coming back.

This was all my fault. Me and him against the world? Well, now the world had split open and swallowed him, taking him away from me.

When I had mostly calmed down, I walked up to the front of the alter where my necklace had fallen. I wasn't ready to look at it yet, much less put it on, but I didn't want to leave it behind. I shoved it in my pocket and stared up at the cross.

"What did I do wrong?" I asked God. "Why did this have to happen? I know You have a plan for me, and that everything you do happens for a reason, but I just don't understand. I don't get what You're trying to tell me. What could be worth all this?"

I didn't have it in me to yell anymore. I was tired of fighting.

Turning on my heel, I left the church, letting the door slam behind me. The fresh breeze felt good on my face, and with one swipe I pushed the tears off my cheeks.

As I walked down the front steps, I was reminded of the night I had met Emerson. I'd been a poor girl, struggling with grief, having lost trust in God. She had been sitting on these steps, waiting for a miracle.

I wanted to believe I'd changed since that day a month and a half ago. But standing here, going through all those same feelings over again, it didn't feel that way. There was no Emerson to swoop in and save the day this time. He was gone, leaving me with a broken heart and an empty promise.

"I'll never leave you."

Those were the words he had promised me the day he had given me the necklace. Tonight he had sworn that he wasn't breaking that promise. Was that true? Maybe I was the one who had broken the promise.

Well, it didn't matter now. Whatever happened next, I would have to do it myself.

By now it was four o'clock in the morning and I didn't want to go home. Instead I came up with a crazy idea.

Jumping up from the steps, I started walking towards a place I had been a million times: Emilio's house. Except his parents didn't even live there anymore; they'd left and moved to Florida.

I didn't care. It would always be Emilio's house to me.

When I got there, I jiggled the handle of the front door and pushed, trying to see if it was unlocked. It was.

Quietly, I tiptoed inside and turned on the light. I hadn't been here in so long, and now I remembered why. Everywhere I looked, there was a memory. But not just memories of just me and Emilio. Memories of Emilio, Ashley, and me.

I sat in the hallway, shaking, and sat down the floor.

"I wish you were here, Emilio," I whispered. "I miss you so much."

I lay my head against the wall, swallowing another round of crying. I didn't want to cry anymore. Instead I sat completely still, taking deep breaths.

After a while, I decided I'd had enough and got up to leave.

Now, no one had lived here for at least four weeks, so it's understandable that I freaked out when I suddenly heard a voice coming from one of the rooms down the hall.

Who could possibly be here?

I ducked into the room next to where the voice had come from, opening the vent in the bottom corner. Through it, I could hear the conversation happening next door.

"Just a little while longer!" the voice said. It was a man, and it seemed like he was talking into a phone. "No, I need you to give it another week. Yes! Because I said so! Things are going according to plan, don't worry. Your time will come… He won't be back any time soon. Seattle. Yes. Be patient, my son."

I heard a beep, then a click, and the room went silent.

My heart was thumping so hard that I was sure the man on the other side of the wall could hear it. Not knowing what else to do, I stuck the vent back in and ran out of the room.

"Hello?" the voice called.

He had heard me!

"Who are you? What are you doing here? I'll call the cops on you!"

I had gotten to the front door, but my hand froze on the handle. That voice seemed so familiar... so...

Just as I was about to turn the handle, I heard the man whisper directly into my ear: "Caught you."

I screamed and fell to the ground, shaking.

"Cadence?" the man asked.

When I looked up, I blinked in shock. It was Emilio's dad! And he didn't at all seem happy to see me.

"Mr. Eastman? What are you doing here?" I asked breathlessly.

What was he doing here? I mean, I knew that he came to check on the house sometimes, since it hadn't sold yet... but it had been ages since the last time he'd been in town, or so I thought.

He stared at me, so surprised that he didn't move. He mouthed some words, but I couldn't read his lips, and within a moment he had ripped open the door and ran outside.

Getting to my feet, I ran after him. I managed to chase him halfway down the block, but then a car's headlights came into view and I was stopped by their blinding light. Mr. Eastman threw open the door on the passenger side and jumped in.

Soon the car sped away and was gone.

I leaned over, trying to catch my breath. Who had he been talking to on the phone? Who had been in the car? I was so confused.

But there was no time to worry about it now.

Totally dazed, I walked home, a million questions swirling in my mind.

———◆———

The next morning, I told my mom about the news Emerson had shared with me at the church, but I left out our fight and my encounter with Mr. Eastman.

Emerson was leaving today, and I had to say a proper good-bye. The previous night couldn't be the last time I saw him. I had been through an ending like that once before, and I wouldn't let it happen again. If I never saw him again, I wanted our last meeting to be happy.

So at ten o'clock in the morning, my mom drove me to Emerson's house just as his mom was locking the door. Emerson was standing in the yard, looking around doubtfully.

"I don't think she's coming, honey," I heard his mom say. "Come now, your dad's waiting."

Emerson sighed dejectedly and was just about to open his car door when I called out his name. He whipped his head around, a smile creeping onto his face.

He left the car door open and ran down the sidewalk. I did the same, meeting him halfway, where I jumped into his arms and threw my arms around his neck. He hugged me tightly, spinning me around until we were both laughing.

His dad honked the car horn, and Emerson stopped spinning me—but he didn't let go. I buried my head in his chest, taking in his smell so I could remember it until he came back.

"Goodbye, Emerson." I whispered up at him.

He smiled, tucking a stray piece of hair back behind my ear and kissing my forehead. "See you soon, Cadence."

Then he broke away from me and got into the car.

I stayed on the street, waving goodbye until he couldn't see me anymore.

Maybe we hadn't fixed everything, and it was still far from perfect. But it was a start, and it would hold us for a little while.

"I know that was hard for you," my mom said to me later in the day once we'd returned home. "But he'll be back. Don't you worry about that."

She gave me a knowing smile and patted my hand. I didn't have the energy to get into it again, though, so I just nodded and didn't push the subject.

"Right. Anyway, can you take me to Ashley's?" I asked.

She sighed, disappointed that I wouldn't say anything about it.

We drove to Ashley's house in silence, both of our minds stuck on Emerson and what was going to happen.

Ashley was outside in her front yard playing with the dog when we pulled up. I took a deep breath and stepped out of the car, waving at my mom as she drove away.

When Ashley saw me, she crossed her arms. The dog just happily chewed on a bone, happy that no one was trying to take it away.

"What do you want, Cadence?" Her tone was tired and upset, like she really didn't want to hear what I had to say.

I pushed on anyway. "I was wondering if we could look at the Emilio box together. Remember, that box I had with all the pictures and letters, notes and memories? You took it from me the week after he died…"

She sighed and dropped her hands, motioning for me to follow into the house. Sunlight streamed in from the living room windows, filling the whole room with natural light.

Ashley had kept the box in the same place I had, in the top corner of her closet. We were soon sitting on the bed, the box between us. Neither one of us opened it. For a minute, we just stared at the photo of him on the front. Happy and laughing and smiling. Like he didn't have a care in the world. That's how I wanted to remember him. As a good person.

She pushed the box towards me. "Would you like to do the honours?"

Smiling in gratitude, I lifted the top off and began pulling things out. As I flipped through some photos, she pointed to one in particular.

"Remember this?" she asked.

The photo was from the time we had gone to the local carnival and Emilio had won us each huge pink teddy bears that were half our size. In the picture we were hugging them with one arm, the other around Emilio, who had a huge piece of cotton candy in his mouth. Behind us was the Ferris wheel, its lights bright and shining in the darkening sky.

"Of course! We had so much fun that day," I said. "Remember when we were on that rollercoaster with the thirty-foot drop that went directly down, but at the bottom it scooped and we went up twenty feet? That was so scary. Emilio screamed so loud, we teased him for weeks."

Ashley burst out laughing. "Oh my gosh, that was hilarious! He could barely talk after that!"

It went on like that for a few photos, one of us retelling the story and the other adding in extra details. We were finally starting to have fun.

That is, until we came to the last photo in the stack. It was the last picture I had taken with him before he died.

"The last day of school," I murmured.

In this photo, we were standing in front of our old elementary school, my head on his shoulder and my arms wrapped around his waist. His arm was around my shoulders.

Ashley wasn't in this one. She had taken it.

"We were so excited because we were going to high school next year," Ashley said. "Our whole lives ahead of us… remember all those big dreams we had? All those crazy things we wanted to do?"

I nodded sadly, staring at my happy, smiling face. Where had that girl gone? That girl who wouldn't let anything stop her, the girl who never put anything before her friends, the girl who had fallen in love with her best friend?

"If Emilio were here now, you know what he would say?" I said. "He would be disappointed in us. We let his death come between us. That's not what he wanted. Remember what he always told us? 'The world is always changing, every second. And most of the time you don't know what's going to happen. But as long as you have good friends who are there for you through it all, you'll always have a place in this world.'"

She nodded sadly, picking up another photo. "So we make things right."

The next photo she showed me was a picture of the two of us when we were eight years old, our arms around each other, sunglasses on our heads and matching hoodies wrapped around our waists. We were standing on the beach, the bright ocean sky and sea behind us.

"This picture was taken the day we promised to be best friends forever," she reminded me.

I looked at the photo again, two eight-year-olds taking on the world together. "We've both made mistakes, Ashley. Can we just accept that and move on?"

She shook her head, tears dripping onto the photo. "Don't you get it, Cadence? It was always you, me, and Emilio. We made it work because we had him. He was our core, the centre. Without him, we don't really have anything. The bottom line here is that we don't know how to be friends without Emilio. He made everything work."

I could tell this was hard for her to say. My heart sank so low that I wanted to crawl under her blankets and never come out.

"Ashley, no! I'm trying. I swear I'm trying! It's still early. We just have to completely heal… then we can work on our friendship again."

She shook her head, wiping at the tears before turning back to me, a sad look in her eyes. "That's the point, Cadence. We shouldn't have to try so hard. It should just work, come naturally. Let's face it. We ran our course. We had a great few years with lots of great memories, but it's time to say goodbye now."

I opened my moth to say something, but I knew she was right. So I hugged her one last time and said goodbye to my childhood friend, the girl who had gotten me through so many hard times in life.

Now we just needed to figure out for ourselves who we wanted to be.

Chapter Eight

What Happened to Goodbye?

"CADENCE, SOMEONE'S AT THE DOOR. CAN YOU GET IT?"

I was in the kitchen, working on a casserole for supper, while my mom called from her bedroom. She was in the middle of an important conference call for work and couldn't come to the door.

I washed my hands and walked to the front of the house. It had been three weeks since Emerson left, and three weeks since the last time I'd seen Ashley, and in that time I had stayed home most of the time. I only went out occasionally; the things I used to do with Emerson just weren't the same without him.

I wasn't sure who was at the door, so I wasn't in a real hurry to get it.

Until I found myself face to face with Emerson.

"Oh my gosh, hi!" I squealed, giving him a huge hug. "Do you want to come in?"

He laughed and hugged me back, kissing the top of my head. I pulled away, standing beside the door so he had room enter.

"So how is Seattle?" I asked once he had sat down on the couch.

"It's good. My parents and I do lots of sightseeing when we're not with Mia. I've been to the Museum of Pop Culture, the Seattle Great Wheel, and of course the T-Mobile Park and CenturyLink Field for a game. It's pretty cool."

I smiled, noticing the way his mood seemed to brighten when he mentioned the baseball field. He was still telling me about it when my mom came out from her room to see who our visitor was.

"Good to see you, Emerson," she said. "Your parents just gave me a call. It seems we'll be joining you at the hotel for dinner. Now, come and give me a hug!"

His face fell when she mentioned dinner, but it quickly changed to his usual smile as he stood up and gave her a hug.

When they parted, my mom turned to me. "Would you like me to finish that casserole for you?"

I nodded.

"Do you want to come outside with me?" I asked.

Emerson shrugged. I couldn't help feeling like something was bothering him, since he wasn't acting like his usual self.

We went out the front door and through the gate that led into our backyard.

"Remember this tree?" I asked. "It's still my favourite spot. Although it's not the same without you. Come, let's go sit up there. For old time's sake."

I climbed halfway up and sat in the most comfortable position, nestled between a branch and the trunk. Emerson followed me up, perching himself on the opposite side of the tree.

We just sat there for a few minutes, saying everything but nothing at the same time.

"How have you been since I left?" he asked. "Have you, you know, talked to Ashley?"

I sighed, staring at the ground. It was a story I didn't really want to get into, but I knew I owed it to him.

"I did talk to her. We were looking at the Emilio box, flipping through photos and stuff. She... she told me that Emilio was the person who held us together. Now that he's gone, she doesn't believe that we know how to be friends. It's just not the same, and it will never be the same. We're not, like, mean to each other or anything... but we won't be friends like we used to be."

Emerson shook his head sadly. "You're going to regret that. Maybe not today, maybe not tomorrow, but one day. You'll regret that you didn't try harder, didn't do more. Because one day she'll be gone. You'll never forgive yourself for not being the person you could have been."

I wasn't sure what he meant about that, whether he was talking about my situation or maybe something else entirely.

"Emerson, are you okay? You haven't been acting like yourself. Did something happen in Seattle?"

He looked up at me, and his expression made me think he really wanted to tell me something. He opened his mouth, then shut it, breaking his gaze and shaking his head.

"That's not... it's just... some hurts go deeper than romantic relationships. Remember that, okay?"

A terrible thought hit me and my gut rolled. I thought I was going to be sick. Was he talking about...

"Are you talking about Mia? I mean, she's okay over there, right?"

His eyes widened, his lower lip trembled, and he didn't say anything for a long time. He just sat there with a faraway look on his face, lost in the land of his own thoughts.

When he spoke again, it sounded like he was holding something back. "No, she's fine. The doctors are taking care of her. Just remember what I said, okay?"

I nodded.

He gave me a smile and leaned back into the trunk. "Good."

For the rest of the afternoon, we sat in that tree. He told me about the cool things to do in Seattle, the baseball players he got to meet... all sorts of things. But soon our time was cut short when my mother came to get us.

"Cadence, Emerson, it's time to go!" she called from the window.

We sighed and made our way down the tree, jumping the last two feet.

———

When we pulled up to the hotel where Emerson was staying, his parents were sitting in the front lobby on the couches. His dad was dressed in his usual outfit of khaki shorts and a colourful Hawaiian shirt. His mother was dressed in a sleeveless purple tanktop and jean shorts, her long straight hair pulled back into a sleek ponytail.

They both looked grim, with tight smiles and sad eyes, but they greeted us with hugs and loose laughter. On our way to the restaurant, our mom chatted with his and I held Emerson's hand. His dad hung back, his hands shoved deep into his pockets. Watching him, I couldn't help feeling like something was wrong.

"So tell us about your move," my mom said once we were seated at our table. She sipped from her glass of red wine. "What is it like over there in the big city?"

Emerson's father answered. He had placed his hand on top of his wife's, and he never moved it once during the meal.

"Well, we've taken Emerson to all the big places he wanted to see, especially the famous ballpark," he said. "The three of us have been to Kerry Park. Much to do there. And my wife and I have spent a few evenings at Wine Country. Fabulous place. I myself have been to the Seattle needle, which has quite the view, I must say."

My mom nodded politely, looking troubled at the mention of only three of them. "What about your daughter? Have you taken her anywhere? I know she probably can't leave the hospi-tal, but—"

I knew she was just trying to be polite, but the comment seemed to really bother them. Emerson's father started blinking hard and focused instead on his beer can, patting his wife's hand. She swallowed and gave my mother a tight smile.

"We also had plans to take Mia to the Seattle Art Museum. But of course, not anymore."

My mother looked back and forth between the three of them, who seemed really upset. Confused, she pressed her hands on the table.

"Why not? Surely, she'll be able to go in a few weeks…"

Emerson's dad snapped his head up, seeming to understand for the first time that we had no idea what was going on. His wife gasped, her lip trembling as she started to take deep breaths, desperately trying to keep herself under control.

His dad glared at Emerson. "You didn't tell them? My boy, that's the reason we sent you there! I didn't want to do this here!"

My mom started sipping her drink again, clearly deciding to stay out of the situation.

But I couldn't. This must be the reason everyone looked so upset, why Emerson had been so distant when he arrived.

"Do what? What's going on?" I asked.

Emerson's mom dabbed at her eyes with her napkin, but waiters arrived with our food just before she was about to explain the situation.

Once they were gone, she clenched the napkin in her free hand, staring at the steaming plate of food.

"Mia… she… well, the move was extremely hard on her condition," said Emerson's mother. "They say, you know, if the situation becomes too severe, it can start to affect other vital organs, like your heart, and… and she died."

Now it was my mom's turn to gasp. She covered her mouth with one hand.

Emerson's mom was crying silently now, his dad clenching the tablecloth, refusing to look at any of us.

As for Emerson, he had his head between his hands, trying to compose the storm that was threatening to come out if he couldn't get himself under control.

I stood up from the table, no longer hungry, and put my hand on Emerson's shoulder. He seemed to understand what I was asking, and he stood up too.

Together we walked out of the dining room and down some hallways until we were standing on the stairs by the emergency exit, far enough away that nobody could hear us.

"I don't understand why you didn't tell me," I said gently, trying to keep my tone soothing. I needed be strong and understanding, for his sake. Isn't that what I had always told him? What kind of person would I be if I made him believe he needed to be strong, but then I didn't do it myself.

He looked upset and tired, all that pain he had been holding back finally coming to light.

"I didn't tell you because you were so happy to see me," he said. "That way your eyes lit up when you talked to me... I just didn't want to ruin that for you."

I just stared at him, a million thoughts racing through my head. He watched as I paced back and forth, until he couldn't take it anymore and slumped onto the steps, tears streaming down his face.

I stood behind him, watching for a moment before deciding that there was no way I could let him go through this alone. So I sat on the step beside him and put an arm around his shoulder. Any anger I'd been feeling melted away into sympathy.

I wrapped both my arms around him and began to cry. "I'm so sorry, Emerson. I could have done something, said something…"

He lifted his head, sniffling. His eyes were red and swollen. "When Emilio died, was there anything anyone could say, anything anyone could do, to make you feel better?"

I shook my head.

Be strong, I thought. *Be strong for him.*

"What do you want me to do, Emerson?" I asked.

"I don't know yet. But you figured it out, right? I'll figure it out too. Somehow."

He stood up and opened the door that led back towards the dining room. I jumped up, catching the door before it closed.

"Emerson, wait! Please!"

He turned and gave me a sad smile, but kept going, looking for a way out. A way to escape the monster called Grief. I knew it would keep chasing him, always on his heels, until he found the courage to turn and face it.

But for now, he was just running.

I hoped with my whole heart that this was the hardest thing we would have to deal with this summer.

———•———

The next day, while lying on the couch eating ice cream and watching TV, I heard a knock on the door. I smiled to myself, knowing it would be Emerson. I was glad he had finally come back to let me help him get through this.

But it wasn't Emerson; it was the very last person I had ever expected to see. The person I had dreamed about seeing for months.

The person who had died.

And was now standing at my front door.

Chapter Nine

Your Secret, My Breaking Point

"CADENCE! I'M SO HAPPY TO SEE YOU!" EMILIO GREETED ME, AN easy-going smile on his face.

"E–milio?" I dropped my bowl of ice cream. It shattered on the floor, ice cream splashing all over the place.

My mom heard the crash and came running out of her room. "What was that sound, honey? Are you okay?"

I whirled around at her, my eyes wide.

She saw the broken pieces of glass and ice cream and was about to scold me when I threw my finger in Emilio's direction.

My mom looked at Emilio and sighed, eyes sad. "You better come in and have a seat, boy."

Emilio lowered a gentle hand on my arm, causing me to jump back and slip in the mess all over the floor. But he caught me before I could fall.

Our eyes met, and that's when I knew this was real. He was really here.

"It's really you," I whispered.

He gave me one of his cute, easy smiles that used to make me feel like the most important person in the world.

Carefully, I navigated my way through the glass to the couch.

"What's going on?" I demanded. "How are you here?"

My mom patted my knee. "Honey, just calm down, okay?"

I stared at her as the reality of the situation finally came together—why my mom hadn't been thrilled about me and Emerson, how upset she had been when Ashley and I stopped hanging out...

My mother had known this whole time.

"You knew! You knew about this!" I accused her.

As I glanced back forth between her and Emilio, she looked at the floor guiltily.

Emilio looked exactly as he had the last time I'd seen him.

"Why?" I asked breathlessly, trying to put everything I was feeling into that one word, trying to make him feel it.

When he didn't say anything, my eyes filled with tears and I ran out the front door.

I bolted toward the bike path, the one that led out of town. Emilio seemed to know where I was going and followed me.

I just wanted to run, but eventually I had to stop because there was a painful cramp in my side. So we walked down the path that led into the countryside so we could be closed off from the rest of town. Closed off from everyone's prying eyes.

"Cadence, what's wrong? Why are you upset?" He sounded hurt, and his expression was the same.

How could he not understand this? Did he think I was going to throw my arms around him like everything could just go back to normal?

"I thought you were dead! I thought you were gone forever! Do you have *any* idea what that was like? After that car crash you were in, the police, the first responders... *everyone* was there! All your buddies made it out with major injuries, but the police were out at the scene for *days* looking for you... after three days, they declared there was no way you could have survived! They pronounced you dead! Dead, Emilio! We couldn't even have a funeral for you because they couldn't find your body in the wreckage!"

He sighed, looking at the ground, like he had just realized things were going to be a lot more difficult than he had anticipated.

"I'm sorry about that, Cadence. Really, I am."

That was all he was going to say? I wiped a few tears away uselessly. "Sorry isn't going to fix this. Don't you get that? Do you understand that the last time I saw you was that huge fight we had? Do you have any idea how that tortured me? What happened, Emilio?!"

He looked grim at the sight of me crying. "Look, this isn't the right time or place to discuss this. I promise I will tell you everything. Just not right now. I'm here now, okay? We can go back to the way things used to be. I'm not going to leave you again."

"Go back to the way things used to be?!" I faced him this time, glaring through my tears. "Things will *never* be the way they used to be! I don't even talk to Ashley anymore. You know why? Because you were the one who held us together."

"Just give me a chance to explain before you go and say something you'll regret. I want to fix this somehow."

I shook my head. Here was the boy I had been in love with, giving me the chance to fall back into his loving arms. And I couldn't take it.

"No, I *can't*. Under other circumstances, maybe I wouldn't hesitate… but when I remember all the pain I went through, I can't help wondering whether this is worth it. When I look into your eyes right now, my heart's no longer broken. And yet I think to myself, maybe I could fall back into this. But no. I can't. Things will never be the same."

I stretched out those last words, trying to make him understand, to see reason.

"Look, just… just calm down, okay?" he said.

He reached out a hand, but I yanked my away aggressively.

"Tell me what happened," I demanded fiercely.

Emilio sighed and ran a hand through his hair, like it would help him come up with some kind of explanation.

"Cadence, now's really not a good time. But I promise I will, okay? Just… give me time."

I stared at him hard, trying to figure out if this was the same Emilio. Why couldn't he understand this?

"You're out of time. You ran out of time a long time ago."

I turned around and started running home.

"Cadence, wait!"

I stopped, squeezing my eyes hard. I had said the exact same thing to Emerson yesterday, only this time I wasn't going to turn around.

I looked up the street towards my house. My mom was standing by the trashcan at the end of the driveway, dumping the broken glass into it.

"What happened?" I asked her. "How could you keep this a secret from me? This whole time, you knew… you knew, and you didn't say anything… How could you let me go through something like that?"

She took it calmly, like she had been prepared for this. I stood there, waiting for her to explain, to say *something*. But all she did was bite her lip and look away.

"How many people knew?" I asked softly.

She looked up, surprised. "Honey—"

"How. Many. People. Knew."

If she wouldn't tell me what happened, I at least needed to know this. I needed to know that I wasn't the only person who had been left in the dark.

"Emerson's parents, Ashley and her mom, and me," she replied quietly.

My stomach clenched and I suddenly felt dizzy. Ashley had known. This whole time.

So many things suddenly started coming together. Why Ashley had been so against me dating Emerson. Who Mr. Eastman had been talking to on the phone; he'd been warning Emilio not to return until the time was right. Why my mom had been so wary of my relationship with Emerson…

"How could you keep this from me?" My voice was hoarse from yelling and holding back sobs. My composure broke and the tears started flowing again.

My mom sighed, tears appearing in her own eyes. "Honey, I didn't know how to tell you. I didn't understand it myself. The night of the car crash, I was taking the back roads on my way to Ashley's house when someone jumped out of the trees, scaring me half to death. I jumped out of my car to see who it was and found myself face to face with Emilio. But I barely recognized him. He was so hurt."

She stopped, taking a deep breath and wiping tears from her eyes.

"Then what?" I asked quietly, still confused as to what this had to do with me.

"He told me to leave, and not to tell anyone that I had seen him," she continued. "We fought, but then he heard a police officer coming and ran off again. I continued on my way and told Ashley's mom what I had seen. We both agreed it was best not to tell you, since we barely understood it ourselves."

I was shaking now, the truth hitting me like a cold front. "But that day when his parents called us over, after the story was released, you all acted like he was dead," I said. "That whole thing was a lie!"

She swallowed, shaking her head. "Emilio was in such bad shape that I believed he was dead, that something horrible had happened to him out there. His parents had been called to the hospital and the doctors said there was nothing they could do. He escaped that night and none of us heard from him again."

My head was spinning, facts and questions swirling around, blocking my vision. I ran into the house and put on my purple hoodie, the one I'd worn when I went to the church with

Emerson in the middle of the night. The memory only made me cry harder.

"Cadence, we just didn't know what to tell you," my mom called after me. "Things were so complicated and mixed up!"

I ran right past Emilio, who had been standing sadly in the driveway. At first I didn't know where to go. Not to Ashley's. Not to Emerson's… he had enough to deal with right now without knowing that my dead boyfriend was standing in my driveway right now…

Instead I went to the church. One inside, I picked the bench where Emerson and I had sat.

Reaching into the pocket of my jeans, I pulled out a necklace, thinking it was the one from Emerson. But instead I realized that it was my locket from Emilio.

Would it be worthwhile to pick up my relationship with Emilio? Would I go through all that again? Did I still want that? I'd changed. Emerson had given me something so great; not only had we built a solid relationship, but we had grown together with God.

I'd never had that with Emilio.

I felt so angry at him for just showing up with no explanation. I felt a burning desire to prove to him how happy I had been without him.

Emerson, Emilio… how could I possibly choose between them?

I was praying to Jesus for direction when the door opened and an old man slid into the bench behind me. He was about seventy years old and was watching me intently, his gaze focused on the two necklaces in my hand.

I was confused. How had I ended up with two? But then I realized one was the necklace Emilio had given me, and the other was the one from Emerson. I must have left it tucked into these pants and forgotten to take it out…

I was about to stuff them back in my pocket when he placed a rough hand on mine, giving me a toothy grin.

"What's the trouble?" He had a kind, soothing voice that calmed me down, even though I didn't know him. Something about this man made me feel like I could trust him.

"It's nothing, really. I just… I had this great boyfriend, then everyone told me he died. So I met this other guy and he just… he gets me in a different way. When I'm with him, I want to be a better person. But now the other guy came back, and he just… he wants everything to go back to normal. He just doesn't understand what I went through, why things aren't the same anymore…"

The guy pulled on the end of his big grey beard. "Well, dearie, it sounds to me like you've made your decision."

I sighed, staring at the necklaces, each one glinting in the light streaming in through the windows.

"But how can I give up on my old boyfriend?" I asked. "We've been through so much! How can I throw away the past two years over someone I met only a few months ago? Shouldn't I trust our history? And I can't give up on the other one… I'm the only one he knows who's been through what he's going through right now. And I owe him for what he did for me."

The man put a hand on my shoulder. "Well, the trouble is that sometimes it takes a big ordeal to realize what you really want in life. If you trust in God, He'll show you the right way."

I nodded, shoving one of the necklaces into my pocket.

"Looks like I'll have to make a decision," I said.

I let out a shaky breath, staring at the one necklace in my hand. I turned away from the old man and put the necklace around my neck.

And when I turned back to thank him, he was gone.

—Chapter Ten—

This Isn't What
I Want Anymore

THE NEXT DAY, I WAS WALKING TO THE LOCAL DINER TO PICK UP dinner for me and my mom when Ashley ran up to me with a huge smile on her face. I had no idea what had gotten her so worked up, until I realized, once again, that she knew all about Emilio being back.

"Cadence, you're never going to believe who showed up at my house last night!"

I tapped my chin, pretending to think. She was so hyper that she was jumping up and down. "Let me guess… Emilio!"

Her face fell slightly.

"He showed up at my house too," I explained. "Did he talk to you about going back to the way things were?"

She nodded vigorously.

"What do you think about that?" I asked carefully, feeling like I already knew the answer.

"Oh my gosh, we should totally do this! I mean, I can't believe he was really alive all this time! I knew he would never give up on us. Aren't you so excited? We can go get ice cream tomorrow, just like old times! And you and I can be friends again. Isn't this great?"

I shook my head. "No, Ashley, it's really not. Aren't you at least a little bit mad at him? And how can you honestly think that things will ever be the same after this? Everything's different now, so no, I'm not excited. And I can't get ice cream with you tomorrow."

I started walking away, but she stepped in front of me, all of her excitement gone.

"What are you talking about?" she said. "Aren't you... aren't you glad to see him again? How can you be mad at him? I can't believe you're saying this. You know, Emilio never deserved you. He makes one mistake, running away from a terrifying experience that scared him out of his mind, running away from all of us, and you can't even forgive him?"

For a minute, I felt bad for what I'd said. The last thing I wanted was to get into another fight, and yet I couldn't just let this go.

"Do you hear yourself right now?" I said. "This is so much bigger than a mistake, and I think it's going to take a lot more than just sorry to fix this. But if this is what you want, then you guys go hang out. I... I just need more time."

I tried my best to keep my voice calm and she seemed to realize that.

"Okay, well, see you around then," Ashley said.

She started walking away, but I stayed put. Something was nagging at me. I couldn't let her walk away without telling her something...

"Ashley!"

She turned around, giving me a confused look, but came back anyway. We stood in silence for a minute.

"How could you know that Emilio was alive and not tell me?" I asked.

Her face fell and she looked like she was about to cry. "I overheard our moms talking about it the night of the accident. I was so sure your mom was lying, that it was all one big mistake. I wanted to tell you, but I wasn't sure. I didn't want to give you false hope. I also wanted to protect you and hold onto that hope that maybe your mom *was* telling the truth."

Hope. There was that word again.

"Okay, thanks for telling me," I replied, giving her a small smile.

I wanted to be mad at her, but I had spent so much time being mad at her that I couldn't stand it anymore. I also needed someone on my side right now.

"Well, when you make the right choice, about giving Emilio another chance, come find us, okay?" she said. "We'll be waiting."

This would be so much easier if I knew what the right choice was. I couldn't just think about myself. It seemed like an impossible choice.

Ashley suddenly pulled back and I turned just in time to see Emilio running up to me.

"I'll let you go," Ashley murmured.

I waved at her as she left, then stepped towards Emilio.

"Hey, Cadence, can I talk to you for a second?" he asked.

He was wearing a pair of long pants and a sweatshirt, despite the heat. Looking at him tonight, realizing that he was really here, I started thinking again that I *could* fall back into this... this way of life where everything was so simple.

"What's up?" I asked happily.

So easy. All my problems could disappear right now.

Dazed, I shook my head. Focus.

He grinned, sticking his hands in his pockets. "I was talking to Ashley this morning, but it looks like you know that already. We were talking about the last two months, and she told me about Emerson."

I let out a breath and rubbed my temples. He looked hurt, like he couldn't believe I would do that to him.

"Emilio, what happened? We had that fight in the rain and you ran off, and I never saw you again. Until yesterday."

I didn't want to fight with him. It hurt so much to fight with him.

He grabbed one of my hands. "I know. So I'm going to explain. That night of the accident, I was with the guys and we were driving home from soccer practice. We were all celebrating, high-fiving, joking around, and having a great time because we'd all made the team. Then Derek, the one who was driving, got a phone call, and he and the Connor started fighting about whether Derek could take the call. Well, Derek wasn't focusing on the phone or paying attention to the road... and he only took his hands off the steering wheel for a second... But the car sped off the road, rolled, and crashing into a tree. When I came to, the first thing I felt was immense pain. The car was destroyed."

I stared at him, my stomach churning at the memory of the images I had seen on the TV.

"I know all of this already," I said.

Emilio looked annoyed. "Then why do you keep asking about what happened?" He

Obviously he still didn't want to talk about this.

"I keep asking because the guy I thought was dead for eight months just suddenly appeared on my doorstep last night, acting like it's no big deal!" I said, raising my voice.

He let out a breath and ran a hand through his hair. As we stood there, I decided that I wasn't going to leave until he told me the truth.

Finally, he picked up the story again. "All I could see when I came to was wreckage. I tried to get up, but I was stuck under a car door. It took me a while to get out, and when I did I felt pain everywhere. I looked around to figure out where we were, but it was too dark out to make anything out.

"Suddenly, I just had this dying urge to get away, and so I started running. I didn't want to get in trouble with the police, and I thought having been in the car might make me some kind of suspect. So I got out of town and called my cousin, who gave me a ride to the hospital a couple of towns over. While I was there, I heard about what was happening back home and the only thing I could think about was getting back to you. But I was still really banged up and they wouldn't let me go.

"After a couple months, I felt fine, so I snuck out and went to my cousin's house. But when the doctors found out, they threatened to call the cops on my cousin. I just... I couldn't get out. Until about a month ago."

My breath caught in my throat. "You mean... this whole time... when we all thought you were dead..."

"I know this looks bad, but what else could I have done?"

I stared at him, shaking my head slowly, biting my lip, anger rolling around in the pit of my stomach

"Emilio, do you have any idea how that sounds? I mean, don't get me wrong, I've been dreaming of this for weeks—for you to come back and make everything better. But I'm not Ashley. I can't just throw my arms around you and forget everything that's happened."

I looked into his eyes—his calm, caring eyes that had gotten me through so many hard times—and noticed his slow smile—the one that could melt me even now—and his shy but confident posture... and for one minute, I wanted to turn off my feelings. Because I hated how much they affected this choice.

I suddenly had a burning desire to look him right in the eyes and say, *"This isn't what I want anymore."* I wanted to ignore everyone else, every logical thought, and just focus on me. What did *I* want?

I stared down the street, towards the house where Emerson lived. I wanted to be with the person who needed me, who let himself be vulnerable one, who made me want to be a better person, and who made me feel like I was enough.

Emilio seemed to realize what I was thinking because he gave me a pleading look. "Look, Cadence, no one can tell you what to feel. But I can tell you how I feel. I love you. I know that you're feeling a million things right now, and what I did is probably unforgivable, but I love you so much. Can't that be enough? We belong together."

I blinked back tears, nodding. He smiled, like that nod had just given him the chance to believe we had a fighting chance. And I wanted to give him a chance, because I had no idea what I would do otherwise. No matter what I did, no matter what I told myself, I would always love Emilio in some way.

———

The next morning, I nervously got ready for my dance class. I knew I would have to tell Emerson that Emilio was back, but I really didn't want to. It was just another heavy thing he would have to bear. It seemed a little cruel to do this to him after his sister had just died.

But he would have to know eventually, and it didn't feel right to keep it from him.

On the way to dance, I prepared a speech. No matter how many times I rehearsed it, though, there was no easy or simple way to say what needed to be said.

When we pulled up to the dance studio, my mom gave me a sympathetic look before letting me out and wishing me luck.

I was a bit late and everyone was already warming up when I got inside. My teacher nodded at me but didn't say anything about my less than perfect entrance. She hated late dancers.

"All right, class, gather around! Today we're going to start with hip hop, then move into salsa, then finish off with some heartbreak ballades. Everyone get into position and we'll start in five."

We all started moving into rows at the same time, finding our usual spots.

Once the music started, I threw myself into it. This was the one part of my day when I got to forget all my problems, my feelings, everything that was pulling me down, and just forget about it. All that mattered when I danced was my reaction to the rhythm of the music. For these few minutes, I became the singer, moving like I had never moved before. The floor was like the surface of a shining lake and I could stay atop it. This was my chance to show everyone how I was feeling, and it exhilarated me.

When the music stopped, I panted for breath and drank lots of water. Soon the teacher caught my eye and smiled approvingly. I smiled back.

She clapped her hands, indicating that it was time for us to find partners. My stomach rolled around as I found Emerson in the crowd.

As I started walked towards him, I realized I still had time to turn around and find another partner. But I would never forgive myself if I did that.

"Hey," he said, his eyes lighting up. "Want to be my partner?"

He seemed to be in a good mood today, which made me feel even worse. I nodded, trying to put on a smile, but he saw right through that.

"What's wrong?" he asked gently.

I looked up into his eyes. "It's... it's... Emilio. He's here. He's... he's not dead."

Closing my eyes, I let out a sigh. That had not come out the way I'd practiced. But it was the truth. The plain, simple truth.

When I opened my eyes again, the expression on Emerson's face was enough to make me want to die. There was so much pain, sadness, anger, confusion... I had never seen him quite like this.

Before he could reply, our teacher clapped twice—the signal to begin.

"What do you *mean* he's back? That doesn't make any sense!" he muttered angrily as the music came on and we began dancing.

I tried to calm him down, begging him with my eyes to stay under control. "I know. He showed up at my door two days ago, telling me all this stuff... and he wants things to go back to normal. He told me he had been so angry with me that day, that he had been drowning in this town, that he'd needed to get away and live his life and find out who he was... I guess he thought it would be better if I thought he was dead, so I wouldn't follow..."

Emerson glared at me, a fire dancing in his eyes. "That sick, twisted... I can't *believe* this is happening. So, what? He thinks he can just show up here and take you back, just like that? Does he even *know* we're dating?"

He had started to yell and we stopped dancing altogether.

"Of course he knows, Emerson. He just doesn't care!"

I hung my head, putting a hand over my mouth. That was the worst thing I could have said.

The whole class had stopped now, and everyone was staring at us.

"Are you actually considering it, Cadence?" he demanded. "After everything that guy put you through, after all those afternoons when I held you while you cried, after *losing faith in God,* you would actually consider taking him back? Do you know how much I care about you? How much I need you? How happy you make me feel? How you can turn my worst day around by being with me? How you're the only person who could comfort me when my sister died? Because you are, Cadence. And if that's not good enough for you, then I don't know what is."

With that, he turned on his heel and stomped out of the dance studio, slamming the door behind him.

—Chapter Eleven—

Please Don't Leave Me

"HONEY, I KNOW YOU'RE UPSET, BUT WE HAVE TO GO NOW," MY MOM called through the closed door of my bedroom.

I hadn't talked to Emerson since dance class the day before, but his parents had phoned my mom and told her they were going back to Seattle today and wanted to give us the chance to come say goodbye.

I knew Emerson wouldn't be waiting for me to show up this time, but I wanted to go anyway. I would take any chance to make things better.

My mom handed me a muffin when I came into the kitchen. We didn't have time to sit down and eat or else we would miss them.

Once we were in the car, I nibbled on my muffin silently, not really in the mood for breakfast.

"It's going to be okay, honey," my mom said. "I'm sure things will be fine between you two when we get there. He can't blame you could for this."

She was trying to comforting. Only problem was that it didn't feel comforting.

"But what if it's not?" I asked. "He could hold this against me for a long time. Things might never be okay between us again. Mom, you need to understand something. Emilio coming back changes *everything!*"

She sighed and didn't say anything after that.

The airport was crowded when we got there, and we had to dodge in and out between big groups of families and carts full of luggage.

My mom pulled out and started texting frantically. We stood off to the side until her phone beeped. Then she grabbed my arm and led me up the stairs and past a bank of huge glass windows through which we could see planes on the runway.

Finally, we arrived at a waiting area with four rows of plastic chairs filled with people waiting to board their flights. We hadn't been sitting for very long before Emerson and his mom came around the corner.

I jumped up, running over to meet them. Our moms gave each other a small smile and sat with each other, letting us talk.

"Emerson, oh my gosh I'm so glad to see you," I said. "I hate that you're so mad at me. Can't you just give me a chance to explain things better? It's not what you think. I swear!"

He stared angrily at the floor. "It was all an act, wasn't it? That fight we had the night before I left… did you make that up so I would leave and never come back? You knew he was alive all along, didn't you? I feel like you were just waiting to push me out of the way…"

I stared at him like I didn't even know who I he was. He wasn't making any sense.

"Do you even hear yourself right now?" I said. "That's ridiculous!"

I stamped my foot angrily, desperation filling my body. I needed to make him understand that this wasn't my fault, that it didn't have to be this way.

"Ha! I'm not making the mistake of trusting you again. Just forget it, Cadence. I'm tired of fighting for you. If you loved me, really loved me, there would be no competition."

I closed my eyes, fighting with every bit of myself to stop myself from sobbing and screaming. He was going through a lot right now, going through a lot of grief, but I began to panic. He couldn't leave me this way...

"Emerson, stop! What happened? What happened to every single thing you said to me?"

I wasn't sure if he heard what I said, because had started to cry.

"You tell me," he said, turning back. "Actually, don't. I'm going back to Seattle. Coming back was a mistake. Bye, Cadence. Have a great life with Mr. Wonderful."

Then he kept walking, just as the loudspeaker announced their flight.

I started following him, but his mom stopped me. "I'm sorry, sweetie. I tried."

As they passed out of view, I cried even more heavily. This couldn't be the end. I couldn't let him leave like this. He might never come back.

There went the boy who had sat beside me on the church steps, the boy who had prayed with me, the boy who believed prayer could heal even the most broken heart. He was the boy who had taken me to the grove of trees outside town and shared his deepest secrets, who had kissed me, who had baked cookies with me, and who had given me that necklace with our names on it believed it was God who had brought us together.

There went the boy who had taken me to church in the middle of the night, who had been with me through so much, who had believed in me when I didn't believe in myself. The boy who had prayed me countless times, who had grieved with me, who had lost his own sister… and even when I couldn't comfort him, I had given him the worst news he would want to hear.

So maybe his mom was right that she'd tried as hard as she could, but I hadn't.

I ran after them, running through people until I caught up to them just before they walked through the gate.

"Emerson!" I called.

He turned just as he handed the flight attendant his ticket. I ran up to him and kissed him softly, a kiss of apology and promise. When I pulled back, I touched my forehead to his.

"The Lord is close to the broken-hearted," I whispered. "Just… remember that. I'll be here for you."

He nodded, swallowing hard as he looked into my eyes. For a minute, I thought he was going to change his mind. That he would forgive me. But then he stepped back.

"Goodbye, Cadence."

In his voice, I heard a promise… A promise that he wouldn't be coming back for friendly visits.

My mom put her hand on my shoulder and steer me out of the waiting area. In fact, she kept her hand on my shoulder until we had reached the car. If she hadn't, I wasn't sure I would have been able to move at all. I could have stood in place, unmoving as people moved past me, for hours.

"I really am sorry, Cadence," she said. "That's not what any of us were expecting. But I'm sure he'll change his mind. I mean, I'm sure of it! Just you wait."

She was just trying to make me feel better, but I wasn't listening. Instead I held my necklace from Emerson tightly, watching it shimmer in the light.

I once read in a book that when you can't make a decision, you should flip a coin. If you felt disappointment by the outcome, you'd know you had secretly been hoping for the other one—and so either way you would know what to do. I had never believed you could make decisions like that. That was like messing with fate.

But right now I wanted to flip a coin, to see it fly through the air and *know* that I was making the right decision.

Once we reached the main part of town, I was leaning my head against the window, my gaze never leaving Emerson's necklace.

She sighed and pulled over to the side of the road. "Honey, I don't think home is a good place for you right now. You need to do something, go somewhere. I don't care what, but just please try and take your mind off what's happened."

I nodded miserably as I opened the door and got out, slamming it behind me.

Before I walked away, she rolled down the window and called me back. "You forgot something."

She passed me a locket, the one from Emilio, then drove away.

Dejectedly, I walked towards the park. It was the one place I had never been with Emerson. I mean, we had been to the park, but only on the side where the play structure was, where we had sat and watched the little kids.

Instead I headed towards the big open field, full of lush grass. I would find the perfect spot to sit under a tree, then lean against the thick trunk, the grass tickling my legs, and be alone with my thoughts.

I hadn't been there for long when a figure came into view, a soccer ball tucked under one arm. He had something tucked under his arm, and as I watched he pulled it out and I realized it was a pop-up soccer net. From my position under the tree, I watched as kicked his ball at the net, practicing neat tricks.

After a few minutes, I got up and walked over. But it wasn't until I was standing in front of him that I realized who it was.

"Emilio!" I exclaimed in surprise. How had I not recognized him? "I didn't know you could play soccer…"

He blushed a bit, pushing the ball back and forth with his right foot. "Yeah, its's something I picked up on my, uh… *trip*."

We both stared at the ground awkwardly, neither of us saying anything for a minute.

Then he perked up and handed me the ball. "You want to play? With me?"

"Sure." I stared at the ball in my hands. "I'm not very good, though."

I followed him into the middle of the field, where I dropped the ball and stepped back.

He smiled. "I'll let you take a few practice kicks."

Every time I kicked the ball, he chased it down and threw it back to me. Most of the time I missed, but on my last hit I got the ball to land right in the middle of the goal.

"Nice!" Emilio called, jogging over to switch positions with me. "Okay, my turn."

He didn't take a running start like I had; he just kicked the ball and it went in. I picked it up and threw it back. On his next two shots, he missed once and scored on the other.

"All right," he said. "Game time?"

"Sure."

I carried the ball closer to him.

"Okay, so we'll go to twenty-one points," he said, explaining the rules. "Goals count as three."

I nodded and dropped the ball in front of us. Emilio immediately took it and started running. I followed, managing to get in front of him and nicking it away from his foot. I kicked it sideways, getting it into the net.

After the goal, we moved back to the centre of the field and went again. This time I had the ball, and he stole it from me and scored.

When he kicked it back towards me, I wasn't paying attention and took it right in the knee.

"Sorry!" he exclaimed as he jogged over.

"It's fine."

We kept playing for a while longer, until one round where Emilio took a power shot closer to the net, missed, and the ball went skidding towards the tree where I was watching. I burst out laughing as he ran after it. Once he came back, he dropped the ball in a new spot, from a ninety-degree angle.

"Come be defence," he said once he'd retrieved the ball and dropped it in a new spot. "Protect your goal from the winning point!"

He pulled his foot back and started running at me. I focused on the ball, trying to take it from him, which he wasn't having. We wrestled back and forth with it, creeping closer to the goal. Soon we were right in front of it and we kicked at the same time… I tripped, causing him to fall too.

We toppled onto the grass, laughing as the ball rolled off. Nobody won the game. Once we had calmed down, I noticed how close Emilio was to me. So close that we were sharing the same breath.

We stayed like that for a minute, just staring into each other's eyes. I had been having so much fun that I'd completely forgotten about our situation. Today had given me proof that we could make things go back to normal, that I could forgive him.

He leaned in close to me and I rested my arms around his shoulders.

But at the last second I pulled away, tears slipping down my cheek.

"I… I can't, Emilio. I'm so sorry."

I gently pushed him away, trying to ignore the hurt look on his face.

When I was at the edge of the park, back at the tree where I had started, I suddenly broke into a run. I didn't stop running until I had found a bench. I sat down to catch my breath, putting my head between my legs.

It took me a while to realize I was on Emilio's street, close to the spot where I had been chasing Mr. Eastman that night when I had gone to his house in the middle of the night.

It seemed clear now that Emilio had always been planning to come back, and yet I had given up on him and turned to Emerson. I felt a little bit guilty, but I also knew it wasn't fair. I had thought he was dead!

Sick and tired of fighting with myself, I started walking again, until both of my necklaces fell out of my pocket and I stopped to pick them up off the pavement. I stopped as I looked down at them, once again thinking about the coin-flipping theory.

Suddenly, I made a decision. I stuck Emerson's necklace in my back pocket and held the Emilio locket close to my chest.

———◆———

I took a deep breath before I knocked on Emilio's door, pacing back and forth across the wooden floorboards of the deck. It had been a whole day since we had played soccer at the park, and after I'd left I had thought of something important I needed to discuss with him.

"Hi Cadence. Can I help you?" his mom asked once I knocked.

I nodded. "Is Emilio around? I need to talk to him."

She sighed quietly, giving me a sympathetic look. "I'll get him for you."

I sat on the railing of the deck and waited until Emilio slipped out the door.

"Hey Cadence," he said with that typical easygoing smile on his face. He wore a loose grey T-shirt and green shorts with a shiny new pair of runners.

I gave him a small smile. "Come for a walk with me?"

We walked in silence for a bit, following the sidewalk that led through the main part of town.

"We need to talk about something," I said. "It's not that I'm not happy to see you, because I am. I'm glad you're here again. It's just that you have no idea what I've been through these past few months. Your death was one of the hardest things I've ever had to deal with."

Tears started welling up in my eyes.

"I know, and I'm sorry, okay?" he said. "Can't we just move past this? I don't want to keep fighting…"

The hurt was visible on his face. It broke my heart to see that.

But I couldn't stop. I had to say this. "I will forgive you. Eventually. I just need some time. This is really hard for me, Emilio. A lot of things have changed. And it's not fair to make you wait around for me, hoping things will go back to the way they used to be. Because at least between you and me, they won't."

Tears spilled out onto my cheeks. The pain I felt made it hard to speak.

Emilio blinked furiously, refusing to look at me as he ran his hands through his hair over and over. "What are you saying? You don't want anything to do with me anymore?"

"I know that you and Ashley have always been really close," I continued. "And you should know that she really cares about you. She told me that you came to see her yesterday, and it sounded like you really care about her too…"

Emilio was quiet for a minute.

"But I can't," he muttered.

I stopped and stood in front of him. "Why not?" I asked quietly, so quietly that I wasn't even sure if he heard me.

"Because of you. What about you?"

I took a deep breath and bit my lip, staring at the ground. I still felt that pull in my gut, that painful pull of sadness that came from knowing that he still cared so much. But I couldn't care for him back, not the same way. And he deserved someone who did.

"Don't worry about me," I said. "It's time you did something else. And Ashley… well, she's so happy you're back, and she doesn't blame you or resent you at all. She just wants to make you happy."

Now it was my turn not to look at him.

Emilio stepped back, taking a deep breath. "I admit, I have thought about it… but Cadence—"

I put my hand on his mouth and shook my head, swallowing back tears that were threatening to come.

"Don't," I said. "She can give you what I can't. If this is what you want, then just say the word. I'll handle the rest."

I held his gaze until he nodded. Then I stepped back and let him go.

———————

Around lunchtime, I walked into Ashley's house. She was in the kitchen, wearing an apron. Flour was dusted on her face and she felt a measuring cup full of something that looked like gravy.

"Taste," she commanded, holding a spoon in front of my mouth.

I bent down slightly and put the spoon in my mouth. "Ash, this is really good!"

She smiled and I stepped closer to the table, which was contained a bowl of cut veggies, rolling pin, cake pan, and mound of dough. Flour covered the middle of the tabletop.

I sat across from her and watched as she dumped the gravy into the bowl of veggies and began stirring it all together.

"What's up?" she asked. "Did you change you mind about Emilio? Are you coming out for ice cream this afternoon?"

I sighed, fiddling with Emilio's locket under the table. She didn't seem to notice. She just ripped off a chunk of dough and started rolling it out.

"I did come here to talk about Emilio, but it's not in the way you think." I paused, lifting the locket and putting it down on the table. "Things won't ever be the same for me. I just can't run to Emilio with my arms open wide and forget everything that's happened. Maybe that's not me… but it's you, Ash. And he deserves that."

She stared wide-eyed at me. "What are you saying, Cadence? You don't want anything to do with us again?"

Her eyes were so full of hurt at the idea.

I reached out to put my hand on hers. "No, that's not what I meant. I still want to be friends with you guys, but I can't forgive Emilio like you can… and I can't fall into our old rhythm. So I'm giving you the locket. Put your own photos in it. Keep the Emilio box. It's your turn to be happy."

"You really mean that Cadence?" She asked, beaming as she spilled the veggie and gravy mix into her pie shell. "But what about you? Are you going to be okay?"

I was about to reach for the locket again, but I stopped myself. It wasn't mine anymore.

"I'll figure something out," I said. "Don't I always?"

She smiled and picked up the locket like it was made of gold. Looking at her now, I knew that I had made the right decision. Somehow I would be all right. Ashley was finally getting the happily-ever-after she had always been chasing. She wouldn't have to feel alone anymore.

I'd had my chance. Now it was her turn.

Once her pie was in the oven, we went out together for a walk. Along the way, we bumped into Emilio.

"This is what you really want, isn't it?" he asked.

He didn't sound angry, or sad, or depressed. It sounded like he would be happy as long as I was happy.

I smiled and nodded.

"Okay, Ashley, what do you say we give this a try?" He smiled, a new light in his eyes that hadn't been there for days.

She beamed and nodded.

Then we all got together for a group hug.

It was official: Emilio wasn't my boyfriend anymore. He wasn't the centre of my world. But he was still important to me, and he would always be special. I would always love him, just in a different way than I had before.

And standing there, hugging my two best friends, I wasn't angry. I knew, deep in my heart, that everything was going to be okay. God had never abandoned me. He hadn't been punishing me. Instead He had taught me what was really important: that you always have to hold onto the people who make you happy, no matter what. Family sticks with us, whether it's our family by blood or the families we make for ourselves.

In that moment, I knew what I had to do to make things right.

———————

"Mom! We have to go! Right now!" I burst through the front door of the house only a few minutes after leaving Ashley and Emilio behind.

My mom came rushing down the hallway, a panicked look on face. "Cadence, are you okay? What's wrong?"

I shut the door behind me, kicked off my flipflops, and changed into runners.

She sighed and plopped down beside me on the couch. "Honey, I know this is hard, but you have to give Emerson some space. There's nothing you can do right now but wait. You have to give him the time he needs to sort things out for himself. You can't do anything about that."

I finished tying my shoes and glared at her. "There's *always* something we can do. What's meant to be will always find a way. Emerson never gave up on me, so what kind of person would I be if I gave up on him? He needs me right now. And that's enough for me."

She sighed as she fiddled with the car keys in her hands. "Is this what you really want? Do you feel God leading you down this path? Now, I know you're thinking about Emerson right now and what you owe him, but if this isn't what you're meant to do, you don't owe him anything. In the end, you have to think about yourself too."

"This is what I want I want, Mom. This is what I need."

She held my gaze for a minute, then slowly nodded. "Okay. I guess we're going to Seattle."

The plane ride took longer than I'd thought it would be, so by the time we were walking out of the airport, donuts and coffee in hand, I was a bundle of nerves. This could be a terrible idea. What if I couldn't do it?

No. I couldn't think like that.

"Where are we going again?" I asked my mom.

She pulled a piece of paper from her pocket, checking the address of the church that Emerson's mom had given her when they'd talked on the plane. Mia's funeral was taking place today.

Soon we were standing on the sidewalk outside a stone church that loomed above us. It had a huge cross at the top and front steps that shone in the afternoon sun. It seemed like a cruel joke that everything about this place seemed so normal and happy when there was a broken and grief-striven family here to mourn the loss of one of their own.

Beside the church was a small graveyard with a white picket fence around it. The grass was neatly trimmed and a small group of people had gathered around a grave in the middle.

Before leaving the airport, my mom and I had changed into formalwear, with me in a knee-length sleeveless black dress that had a slight puff that hung around my body. My hair was curled and my feet were pushed up into black strappy heels. My mother wore a black pencil dress, with slip sleeves that hung on her shoulders and tightened under her neck, sparkly black flats, and a tight, sleek ponytail.

I looked over at her, a knot forming in my stomach. She put an arm around my shoulders, hugging me from the side.

"It's going to be okay," she whispered.

I nodded, closed my eyes, and took a few deep, shuddering breaths.

Before I could change my mind, we stepped through the gate that led into the graveyard. From there we went our separate ways, as she went to find Emerson's mom and I began to look for Emerson.

After silently searching the crowd for a few minutes, I spotted him close to the group, his head bent down in a silent prayer.

"Umm… hi Emerson."

He lifted his head and stared at me, eyes wide. They were full of sadness and grief, red and puffy, with tears rolling down his cheeks.

I tried for a small smile, but he turned away.

"What are you doing here?" he asked gruffly. "You should go. I don't want you wasting your time here when it's something you clearly don't want."

I had been hoping that maybe he wasn't mad anymore, that he might have put the whole thing behind us.

"Emerson—"

"Look, thanks for coming." He wiped angrily at the tears that kept falling, no matter how much he tried to keep them away. His pain demanded to be felt. "It's nice of you to support my sister and everything, but I don't want you here. I'm going through enough right now. The last thing I want is to get into another fight with you. So please just leave, okay?"

I didn't say anything. I didn't move. He stared towards the front of the group, ignoring me. My presence seemed to unnerve him.

"Why do you keep pushing me away, Emerson? I know it feels that way, that I don't know what you're going through, but I want to help you."

He ran a hand through his hair, staring off into the distance. He didn't seem able to focus on one thing for too long.

"I don't need your help," he said.

I ran one hand down his arm, like I used to do all the time. I looked up into his eyes. "Everyone needs a little help once in a while."

We were close now, and for a moment I thought he was going to accept my touch. Maybe we would be able to go back to normal...

But then a thought crossed thorough his face and he pulled away. "Cadence, I know you mean well, but I can't be around you when you're with that other guy. So can you please just leave and help me be the better person?"

I swallowed, trying hard not to cry. I wished he would stop and let me help him, but it seemed that every time he got close something pulled him back.

"No," I said. "I'm not going to leave."

He blew out a frustrated breath, kicking at the ground and shaking his head. I knew I had annoyed him, but I didn't exactly care at the moment. All that mattered right now was making things better. I wouldn't be able to forgive myself if we stayed broken forever—two people who had fallen in love for a little while but got torn apart by tragedies.

"Why not?" he asked. He sounded more confused than mad, like he couldn't understand what I felt the urge to stay with him.

I looked up into his eyes again, resting my hands on his chest. "Because you never once gave up on me the whole time I was grieving. You led me back to God and showed me how to be a better person. I have to do the same for you."

He carefully put a hand on my arm, contemplating it. "But what about Emilio? I can't compete with that kind of history. What you two have, it wouldn't be right for me to wreck that."

"You don't have to," I said.

I pulled my hand away and reached into my dress pocket. I held out the necklace he had given me.

He reached out and touched the engraving of our names, a small smile creeping onto his lips.

"When Emilio disappeared, something changed in me, something changed in him, and we moved on," I added. "No matter how much he tries, things will never be the same. And that's okay. We will always be friends."

Emerson smiled for the first time in a long while. He took the necklace from my fingers, opened the clasp, and slipped it around my neck.

"Everyone can now come up and give their offerings," said the pastor at the front. "These offerings will be buried with the deceased."

People around us started moving, pulling things out of pockets and bags.

"What are you giving her?" I asked.

He reached into the inside of his jacket pocket and handed me a silver bracelet with thirteen colourful charms dangling on it. Mia's charm bracelet. He let me hold it, and as soon as it hit my fingertips I started crying.

"Sorry," I mumbled, wiping at the tears and trying to control myself.

Emerson just put his arm around me as we got in line. "Don't be sorry. I think in this case neither of us has to be the strong one. Just don't let me lose sight of what's important again, okay?"

I laughed a little, wiping at my tears. "What makes you say that?"

"Well, I met a really smart girl once who told me that the Lord is close to the broken-hearted, and I figure this is one of those times."

As we walked up to the gravestone and dropped the bracelet in, we stood hand in hand and said a small prayer together. I felt like I had done my job.

Chapter Twelve

A Toast to New Beginnings

"You know, I'm really going to miss her," Emerson muttered as he stared into his cup of punch.

We were sitting on the back steps of the church, the hum of people behind us. After the ceremony, everyone had gathered in the church for sandwiches and drinks. Only a few people had come and give Emerson hugs, professing their sympathy, before he had needed to get out of there.

"We all are," I replied sadly, fiddling with the end of my dress. My punch and plate of fruit sat untouched beside me.

Emerson nodded, blinking back more tears. He silently reached for my hand and interlaced our fingers. Comfort. He needed the comfort of feeling that I was still here with him.

"I just wish… I mean, my parents and I had so many dreams for her. She was going to be an artist. She was going to sell her paintings for millions of dollars, because she was *good*. Her laugh, her smile, the joy that just radiated from her when she entered a room that made you feel good… how are we going to go back to the way things used to be without that?"

I stared at the steps. The afternoon sun shone on them, making them warm.

"Things will never be the same, Emerson. But one day things will start to slowly change, and maybe they won't be exactly the same, and you'll still really miss her, but it will get better and you won't feel so lost anymore. The one thing you can't do, though, is live in the land of what-if. Trust me. It's only going to make you crazy!"

He gave me a confused look and took a sip from his cup. "The land of what-if? What's that?"

I picked up two grapes from the plate, popping one in my mouth and one in his.

"It's like this," I explained. "When I thought Emilio had died, the only thing I could do for a long time was think of all the things I could have said, all the things I could have done differently. Maybe I could have made things right. Emerson, you have so many good memories of your sister. If you don't focus on those, you'll go crazy."

He nodded sadly, stealing another grape from me. "What am I going to do, Cadence?"

The look on his face was so genuine, almost as though he was counting on me to lead him through the crisis. Well, I would give him the best answer I could. It might not be what he wanted to hear, but it was what I needed to say.

It was the reason I hadn't been kiss Emilio while we were playing soccer. It was the reason things couldn't ever be the same between us again. And it was the reason I had flown out here.

"Well, you'll always have me," I said. "For I am convinced that neither death, nor life, nor angels, nor rulers, nor things present, nor things to come, nor powers, nor height, nor depth, nor anything else in all creation, will be able to separate us from the love of God in Christ Jesus our Lord."

He smiled, a true and genuine one. "Romans 8:38–39?"

I smiled, staring at our intertwined hands. I was about to say something further when Emerson's dad poked his head through the back door, sounds from the party crowding out the silence.

"Party's over, guys," he said. "Emerson, can you please come help clean up? After, of course, you say goodbye to Cadence. Her mother's waiting for her."

Emerson nodded and his dad closed the door again.

He sighed, looking sad again. "I guess this is goodbye then."

"Not forever, though. My mom and I are staying for a while. You have to take me on an official tour of the city, since you're now the expert."

My dress swirled as we stood up. Emerson chuckled and wrapped me in his arms, holding me close for those few moments.

"Oh, I almost forgot!" I exclaimed, pulling back.

He frowned. "What?"

I gave him a weak smile and pulled a folded piece of sketchbook paper from my dress pocket. Emerson's breath caught as he unfolded it and saw the drawing.

"Where did you get this?" he asked, staring at me in amazement.

"Mia. She gave it to me that day in the hospital. She said she wanted to paint it and surprise the family. That's why she went to the store that night when she collapsed. She told me that if anything happened to her, I was to give you guys this drawing."

Emerson's eyes filled with tears as he held the picture carefully, like it might shatter at his slightest touch. "You've had this all this time?"

I wasn't sure if he was mad or not, so I started babbling defensively. "Well, I wanted to tell you... but it didn't seem right at the time. You were already so upset about moving, and her illness was a huge strain on your family. I didn't want to make it worse. Before our big fight, I had thought about framing it or something... but then you left and—"

But I was cut off by his lips. His kiss was warm and gentle and thankful. My fingers drifted to his hair and down his back.

When he pulled away, he put his forehead against mine. I bit my lip, looking up into his eyes and giving him a half-smile.

"Thank you, Cadence," he whispered, looking into my eyes. He looked so pleased.

"Just promise me one thing, okay?"

He looked surprised but nodded.

I reached for the picture, which featured every member of his family, and held it up to him. "Promise me you won't give up on these people, okay? They need you, whether you believe that right now or not."

Looking back down at the picture, my gaze lingered on his smiling face.

"Especially not this one," I murmured. "At the end of the day, nobody knows you better than yourself."

He took the picture back and stared at it one more time. After placing it in his pocket, he gave me one last kiss, took my hand, and led me around the church so we could walk past the graveyard, saying one last goodbye to his sister. I gave him a side hug, like my mother had done, and suddenly wondered if she had known the whole time that things would turn out this way, that I would do what was right in the end.

Once we walked back to the entrance of the church, the doors were open and only a few people were left. I started helping with the clean-up, giving Emerson a chance to talk to them, to accept the comfort he had been holding back.

As soon as everyone was gone, it was just the five of us again. His parents sat in chairs with sad expressions while my mom talked aimlessly next to his mom.

I shook my head and made my way over to them.

"Everyone, stand up." I commanded.

They all gave me a startled look. My mom seemed to warning me, *"These people are going through a lot right now. I don't think they would appreciate a joke."* But I ignored her and started pulling Emerson's parents up out of their seats. I organized everyone into a circle, then took a place in the open spot beside Emerson and my mom.

"What are you doing exactly, Cadence dear?" Emerson's mom asked, looking a little flustered.

I smiled at her, putting my arms around my mom and Emerson. "A group hug."

Everyone relaxed and we got close together, everyone's arms around each other, Emerson's mom's head on his dad's, and Emerson's on his dad's.

"We're all going to be okay," I said. "You guys will get through it, with the help of God and each other. Each of one of is going through some kind of challenge. And we're all going to be all right."

And standing there, looking into everyone's faces, I truly believed that was the truth.

About
the Author

Ariena Vos is an author with a passion for sharing stories that make you feel. She is passionate about love and emotion and likes to explore these themes and make them come alive in her writing.

Currently, she is working on a sequel to this novel, called *Pieces of a Dream*. Both will be part of the larger Heart of Truth series. She's also working on another emotional romance, called *Each Part of Me*.

She enjoys reading, biking, painting, art, baking, spending time with friends, playing her flute, volunteering, and of course writing! She lives on an alpaca farm with her family outside Avonhurst, Saskatchewan.

To learn more about Ariena Vos, follow her on Instagram at @ariena_1101.

CPSIA information can be obtained
at www.ICGtesting.com
Printed in the USA
LVHW020912111121
702990LV00017B/254

9 781486 620944